"Trueman paints a vivid story of three desperate teens that recalls Robert Cormier, with its dark, disturbing theme and a narrative that shifts from one plot thread to another in rapid-fire succession. Fans of Cormier will likely enjoy this psychological and gripping tale."—*Publishers Weekly*

"A quick and riveting read. Will give readers a memorable if perturbing insight into mental illness."—*KLIATT*

"The events unfold with an edge of danger that provides riveting suspense . . . a plot line that grabs and doesn't let go."—*Kirkus Reviews*

". . . Trueman sometimes captures moments of heartbreaking truth, and his swift, suspenseful plot will have particular appeal to reluctant readers."
—ALA *Booklist*

Wing-wong—

ALSO BY TERRY TRUEMAN
STUCK IN NEUTRAL
CRUISE CONTROL

Robber-snobber .

TERRY TRUEMAN

HARPERTEMPEST

AN IMPRINT OF HARPERCOLLINS*PUBLISHERS*

Inside Out

Library of Congress Cataloging-in-Publication Data
Trueman, Terry.
    Inside out / Terry Trueman—1st ed.
        p. cm.
    Summary: A sixteen-year-old with schizophrenia is caught up in
the events surrounding an attempted robbery by two other teens who
eventually hold him hostage.
    ISBN 0-06-623962-1 — ISBN 0-06-623963-X (lib. bdg.).
    ISBN 0-06-447376-7 (pbk.)
    [1. Schizophrenia—Fiction. 2. Mentally ill—Fiction. 3. Juvenile
delinquency—Fiction. 4. Suicide—Fiction. 5. Hostages—Fiction.]
I. Title.
PZ7.T7813 2003   2002151604
[Fic]—dc21   CIP
                                                              AC

Typography by Andrea Vandergrift
11 12 13 14   CG/CW   10
❖
First paperback edition, 2003
Visit us on the World Wide Web!
www.harpertempest.com

For Eric John

quish-wish, squish-wish, bet you wish you could squish a wish!

. . . long gone . . . long gone . . . Gong wong-wong gong

ACKNOWLEDGMENTS

First and foremost, thanks to Antonia Markiet, my brilliant, patient goddess of an editor! Toni helped me craft *Stuck in Neutral*, my first novel, and now we see the birth of a second. Without Toni's help these books would, quite simply, not exist—so "thanks" is an inadequate word to cover the depth of my appreciation to her.

Thanks also to my family, especially Patti Nasburg, Jesse Trueman, Sheehan Trueman, Cindy and Garren Mayer, Bill and John Egger, and Wally and Kathy Egger. Thanks to Dr. Kent Berney; Stacie Wachholz, my manager; my agent, George Nicholson, at Sterling Lord Literistic Inc. and his assistants, past and present—particularly Paul Rodeen. Thanks to the students and staff of the Step-Star satellite schools program and especially to Peggy Yurik; to Tami, Chad, and Godson Ben Gardner; to Terry Davis, Chris Crutcher, Kelly Milner Hall, and Michael Gurian, great writing friends, and to my great friends and supporters at HarperCollins Publishers, notably Phoebe Yeh, Bill Morris, Catherine Balkin, and Josette Kurey.

A special thank-you to YALSA and ALA for the great boost they have given my writing career. In my acknowledgments to *Stuck in Neutral* I listed a lot of the people who helped me. There really are so many more on the list now that now I'm forced into this group thank-you to all of you. I hope you know who you are and how indebted I am.

Wing-wong wing-wong

'Cause you're a gong—wong is a gong, gor

"You're worthless," Dirtbag says.

Zach tries to ignore him.

But then Rat. "You need to die, Wasteoid!"

Zach stares at the rifle he holds in his hands, and he takes a deep breath, slowly turning the weapon toward himself.

"Yeah, die, Wasteoid," Dirtbag says, almost like he's whispering something sweet and kind, almost like he is Zach's friend.

"DIE!" screams Rat.

Zach hesitates, thinks about his mother for just a moment, and then looks at the rifle again. He cocks the weapon and lifts it up, taking the muzzle into his mouth. . . .

a wong. Yes, yes, yes . . . end it all!! Long gone . . . long gone . .

1

All I want is a maple bar, but I don't think these kids with the guns care about what I want.

I didn't even look up when they first walked into the coffee shop, even though the little bell on the door went *tingaling*. But now I look.

"This is a robbery," yells the taller, older-looking kid, holding a black gun. He's around my age, maybe sixteen. The other kid's hand is shaking, and the little silver gun he's holding is shaking too; he looks younger than the first kid.

They both look mad, mean, too.

"We're just here for the cash registers," yells the older kid. "You all just sit tight!"

I glance out the window, and I see a lady in a blue car. Her mouth has dropped open and she's staring straight at us. Now she's talking on her cell phone as she speeds away. I look back at the robber kids. I don't think they saw the lady in the car.

I look around at everybody else in this place, and they all look scared, so I'm trying to look scared too. I mean, I guess I'm scared, but this all seems so normal to me. The thing is, I'm used to seeing and hearing really weird stuff, so this doesn't feel that strange to me at all. It feels familiar. But it's probably weird to everyone else, 'cause they're freaking out.

The two suits sitting over at the table against the wall are white as ghosts. One of them is fat; I don't want to be rude, but he is. His white shirt is stretched tight over his big belly, and his tie doesn't reach his belt. The other one is skinny. They remind me of these two old movie characters, Laurel and Hardy, who were a skinny guy and a fat guy too. Laurel and Hardy are my favorites because they're always arguing and the fat guy yells and the skinny guy starts bawling like a baby. But the fat suit here in this coffee shop isn't yelling, and the skinny suit isn't crying . . . at least not yet.

Two old ladies sitting at the table next to the two suits are quiet and sit very still. I have to stare at them for a few seconds to be sure they're even real. Finally one of them blinks, but I'm still not sure about the other one. The girl and guy who work behind the counter are frozen like statues. Even though I sit in here every day after school waiting for my mom, I don't know the guy's or girl's name and they don't know mine. A lady and her little daughter, who were ordering drinks when these kids with the guns busted in, are just standing with their faces all squinched up, which is too bad because the lady is pretty and her little girl is cute. They could be in a commercial about pretty moms and daughters.

One of the kids with a gun, the older-looking one, says, "Nobody's gonna get hurt if you just do what we tell you!"

I say, "Okay."

He seems surprised at the sound of my voice and looks at me real fast, then away again.

He says, "We don't wanna hurt anybody."

"Good," I say.

He looks at me again, "You got a problem?" He asks. I *think* he sounds mad.

"Yes," I say.

This surprises him too. "Oh, yeah?" he asks. Then he points his gun right at me. "What's your problem?"

I'm sort of surprised that he wants to know.

His gun is big and black, with a wide hole in the end of the barrel. It's like a tunnel.

I answer him as truthfully as I can. "I'm sick, that's my problem; I take medicine two times every day, thanks for asking."

The younger kid yells, "Shut up or we'll hurt you." He sounds like kids at school sound just before they do something like knock your lunch tray out of your hands.

I think about what the older kid said, about not wanting to hurt anybody, so now I'm confused by the younger one saying they might hurt me. "I thought you didn't wanna?" I ask.

"Didn't wanna what?" asks the older kid.

"Hurt anybody"

"We don't." He hesitates. "So don't make us."

"Make you?" Now I'm *really* confused. Why would I try to *make* anybody hurt me? What am I gonna do, say something like "Come on, please, please, shoot me a few times"? And people call *me* weird?

The older kid says, "So just shut up and we *won't* hurt you."

"Ohhh," I say. "Okay." I think, Close one, Zach, you almost screwed up again.

"Zach, you're a stupid wong-gong, a long-gone wong-gong."

I ignore this, but while I'm sitting here being quiet, my palms are sweaty and my throat is dry. I need to decide if this situation is real or not; I need to decide that right now. Sometimes I understand what's going on, and other times I don't have a clue. If I don't figure this one out, I could be in trouble.

So I look closer at the kids with the guns—they're not much bigger than I am. They're both wearing blue jeans and the older one is wearing a baseball hat and a black T-shirt. The younger one doesn't have a hat on and his T-shirt is yellow. Their faces look pretty normal: noses, eyes, mouths, ears and hair and eyebrows. So far so good. If I were just imagining them, they'd probably be missing some of those parts. So I think that probably I'm not imagining them. I think these are real kids with real guns. After all, it looks like the other people sitting here see them too. Dr. Curt always tells me to use all my senses when I'm trying to figure out "reality." Like if I'm hearing too much stuff and my ears are being used up, then I need to use my eyes and nose, my sense of taste and touch to figure if things are real or not. But sometimes I can't trust any of my other senses either.

The thing is, *I* am not normal. I'm *not*, and I can't help it. I get massively confused. I've got two psycho-killer enemies named Dirtbag and Rat after me. My body, most of the time, feels like a foreign country. Like I told the kid with the big black gun, I'm sick.

"Hey, Zach, think, think, shrink shrink, wong-gong."

And then, of course, there's that crap.

I mutter back, "Up yours."

The younger kid points his gun right at me and says, "I thought we told you to shut up!"

"Yeah, you did, really, honestly, you did tell me that," I say. "You said shut up and no one will get hurt." I'm surprised he forgot.

"So why are you still talking?" he demands. Maybe this is one of those times when someone asks a question but doesn't really care about the answer. He's not really *expecting* me to answer. I better shut up just to be safe.

"Hey, Zach, wing-wong, wing-wong, long gone."

This bounces around from one side of the room to the other. I know that no one else can hear this— no one else ever does. I glance at the two businessmen across from me. The skinny one just stares at the table; he looks pale and he's shaking. The fat one looks like *he* would shoot me if he had a gun. Somehow I always make people mad. I don't know why.

I point over at the fat suit, and I say to the robbers, "Does he look mad to you?" The robbers, both of them, turn and look, pointing their guns at him.

The older kid asks the fat suit, "Are you a hero? You gonna give us a problem?"

When the fat suit opens his mouth to speak, his words squeak out of him. "No way! No, sir!" He looks back at me again, his face all twisted up, his mouth pinched real tight and his eyes bulging even more than before. I can't tell if he's sorry or if he wants to kill me.

When I look at other people, I usually don't know what they're feeling. Hell, most times I can't tell what *I'm* feeling—how am I supposed to know what's happening with anybody else? It sure would be good to know though, especially right now.

The older kid turns back to me. "Just try to shut up, okay?" he says. Then he adds, actually sounding kind of nice, loud enough for everybody to hear him, "We'll be done here in just a second, then you can all go home."

When he says this, I glance at my watch and I know that won't work for me. I say, "My mom won't be here till three thirty." I look at my watch again. "It's only three twelve. I have to wait for her."

The older kid says, "Okay."

I say, "I can't leave until she comes to pick me up."

He shifts his gun a little in his hand and says, "Yeah, okay, that's fine. You can stay here until three thirty and wait for her."

I say, "Yeah, I gotta wait here. I can't be home alone anymore, even though she got rid of our rifle. So this is where she meets me. She picks me up here every day after school, then I take my medicine right away. I have to—"

"SHUT UP!" the younger kid screams.

The whole room jumps, even the statue ladies.

His words echo. *"SHUT UP—SHUT UP—SHUT UP—SHUT UP!!!!!"*

I do it. I shut up right away.

The older kid says, "You've gotta be quiet, okay?"

I nod my head yes, so that I won't have to be talking.

"Wing-ding, long gone, your mouth is stupid but you got a long dong."

I ignore this, even though I hate it when anybody talks about my dong.

The younger robber yells at the girl behind the counter, "Hurry up!" As she takes the money out of the cash register, she tries to move her hands faster, shoving the bills into one of the white paper bags they use for giving you maple bars and stuff.

I love maple bars.

Suddenly three cop cars screech to a stop right outside, their lights flashing: red and blue, red and blue, red and blue.

"Wahooo!"

The two kids with the guns start yelling, "Everybody up!" "Hurry up!" "Move it now!" "NOW!"

We're all up and moving so fast that we bump into each other as the robber kids shove us toward the back room—I glance back at the maple bars; I really want one bad—and I notice out the window the cops jumping out of their cars with their guns. The robber kids look freaked out—their eyes are huge and scared, the older one's face is sweaty, and the younger one's face is real red.

The older kid yells, "Hurry up!" and pushes the fat suit, who stumbles and knocks into the lady and her little girl. They bump into one of the old ladies, who almost falls. I wonder if any of us will ever meet the president of the United States. That's stupid, isn't it? I mean, why would we? I trip as the younger robber shoves me hard in my back; I bump into the skinny suit. This is like a kindergarten fire drill, only all of us are lots taller than little kindergarten kids would be— that's stupid too, isn't it? I mean, of course we're taller than kindergartners. I guess I look and act stupid a lot of the time. Lots of people say that to me, so it's probably true.

In another few seconds we're all crammed into this tiny back room of the coffee shop, the part in the back that you never see. I keep thinking how much farther away I am from getting a maple bar— Damn, I hate that!

2

*Dr. Cal Curtis—Medical School Training
Notes:*

Psychotic mental disorders, such as
schizophrenia, affect the way people
understand things and how they act in
social settings. Sometimes these patients
grasp what is happening around them, but
most of the time they get very confused;
they can be aware one moment and unaware
the next. . . .

I wish I had one of those maple bars. If I were a robber, I'd take the money AND the maple bars!

"*Squish-wish, squish-wish, bet you wish you could squish a wish!*"

Maybe I would if I knew what the hell that meant.

"*Wasteoid!*"

I know what THAT means, but lucky for me, it's not Dirtbag or Rat. I *hate* when they show up.

The kids with the guns make us all sit on the floor.

The younger kid peeks out the door at all the cops

and cop cars, then turns back to the older kid and says, "What are we gonna do? What are we gonna do?! The cops are all over the place—they'll blow our heads off—"

The older kid interrupts, "They won't. Just relax. We got all these people in here with us. The cops don't want them to get hurt, so they won't do anything." He pauses a second, then says to all of us, "Just sit there and shut up and you won't get hurt."

I want to stay quiet; I want to relax. But I can't help myself. "What's your names?" I ask.

The older kid looks at me. "You don't want to know our names," he says.

"Yes, I do," I say back. "Otherwise I don't know what to call you."

"Dang!" says the younger gunman. "We had to pick a place with a retard in it?!"

The older kid turns to the younger one and says, "Chill." The older kid turns to me again and says, "You can call me Frosty and him Stormy, okay?"

"Wow," I say, really impressed. "Neat names. Are those your real names? What're your last names? Are you brothers? Wouldn't it be cool if your last name was Day, you know, like Frosty Day and Stormy Day. . . ."

There's a loud sound outside the building, out in

Squish-wish

front. It's more sirens from more police cars.

The older kid, Frosty, ignores the new police sounds and looks at me funny. He asks, "What's wrong with you?"

I say, "I'm not retarded."

Stormy laughs and says, "Yeah, right."

I say, "No, honest, I'm not. Actually, I'm pretty smart. Like ask me anything about school subjects, like math or history. Ask me the number of any president."

I wonder if the president of the United States is here right now. That's stupid again. He's out trying to protect the free world—by the way, what's so free about the free world? I mean, everything I see costs money.

I say, "Come on, just pick any number of president between one and forty-three."

Frosty doesn't think about it for very long. "Seventeen." He's looking out the door again.

"Seventeen," I say. "Andrew Johnson, seventeenth president of the United States of America. Assumed office upon the assassination, by John Wilkes Booth, of the sixteenth president, Abraham Lincoln—"

Frosty interrupts me, "Okay, you're *not* a retard, but just shut up, okay? I've gotta pay attention or someone could get hurt for real."

There're more sounds of policemen yelling things to each other and running around outside.

"Okay," I say.

Frosty pauses for a few seconds, then says to all of us, "We don't want to have to kill you, okay? We want to try and get out of this, so do what we say, when we say it, and just shut up."

When Frosty says the thing about killing us, the little girl sitting with her mom starts to cry. She's really a cute little girl, a lot smaller than her mom. That's another stupid thing to say, isn't it, but that's what I notice, she's little and her mom is bigger. Anyway, the little girl is cute, but I think she's real scared. I remember being scared when I was little, before I got sick. I don't get scared now. As the little girl's crying, her face is all scrunched up and her lips are quivering. Her hands are shaking too, little hands with blue finger-nail polish—yep, she's scared.

Stormy looks down at the little girl and says to her, "Hey!" When she looks up at him, he says, "We're not gonna hurt you, I promise."

The little girl smiles at him, and he smiles back at her.

While I'm sitting here shutting up, I'm thinking

about not understanding things faster. I guess in a way I'm embarrassed about it, but I'm happy to still feel embarrassed—Dr. Curt says a lot of people with my kind of brain don't have feelings at all. He says that would be worse. I guess if he says so, it must be true. One thing for sure, though, I got it bad enough the way I am now, I don't need "worse."

Stormy asks Frosty again, "How're we gonna get outa this?" His voice is shaky.

"I don't know," says Frosty.

Stormy says, "But what about Mom? What about—"

Frosty interrupts. "Just shut up a second, okay? Just chill."

"But . . ." Stormy begins, but when he looks at Frosty, he stops talking.

Suddenly there're more loud sounds of cops outside yelling. Frosty and Stormy look up at each other but don't say anything.

We're all so crowded together, but it's okay, 'cause I'm sitting next to one of the old ladies, who has on some perfume that smells really nice.

"You smell nice," I say to her.

She tries to smile at me, but her mouth can't quite make it. She has kind of pink-purple hair and real wrinkly skin. I mean *really* wrinkly. I wonder if she's a hundred years old. Stupid again, hardly anybody's that old.

So I ask her, "How old are you?"

Stormy says to me, "Jeez, *please*—shut up!"

I forgot I wasn't supposed to talk, or maybe I thought that just counted out in the other room near the maple bars. I guess it counts here, too.

"Oops," I say.

Frosty says, "It's okay. Just try and be quiet, all right?"

I nod.

Frosty kind of half smiles at me, but he can't get his mouth to make a smile any better than the old lady could a few seconds ago. I guess he's scared too.

There's a lot more noise outside the coffee shop. Policemen yell things to each other and their sirens blare and people holler. There's the regular traffic sounds that I always notice when I'm waiting here for my mom, but now there's police radio sounds, running footsteps, and some *beep-beep-beep* sounds, like when a truck is backing up.

"*Wing-wong—wing-wong—wong-gong.*"

I wonder if the feeling I'm feeling right now is fear?

It's hard for me to know what feeling is "appropriate" with what's going on. I'm not appropriate sometimes. Sometimes I'm "inappropriate."

"*Wong-wong—sing-song—Wasteoid—wong-wong.*"

Suddenly I hear this clicking sound. *Click, click, click*. At first I'm not sure where it's coming from, but when I look around, I see that it's Stormy's gun. Stormy is pulling the hammer on his gun, the thing you cock it with, back with his thumb, then easing it back down, over and over again. Every time he pulls it back, then eases it forward, it goes *click*.

I look at the gun for a while, then up at Stormy's face.

He's staring right at me.

I've been on the other end of a gun before. I didn't like it much then—I still don't.

3

*Clinical note by Dr. Cal Curtis on Zachary
M. Wahhsted: First psychotic episode, two
years ago:*

Zachary is a 14-year-old Caucasian male
apprehended while walking barefoot by the
Spokane River on a freezing winter night.
Police reports state that Zachary appeared
"lost and confused" and told them that he
was "afraid of zombies." Zachary further
stated that the mental health professional
who initially interviewed him was "a
zombie in a red sweater."
Initial diagnosis: Schizophrenia,
adolescent onset, paranoid type.

Thinking about it, I realize Frosty and Stormy are probably nicknames, kind of like Wasteoid. I wish I were called Frosty or Stormy. Especially Stormy— that'd be so cool.

But most kids call me Wasteoid. A lot of kids see me as a wasteoid, you know, worthless. Heck, I sometimes feel that way about myself, too, especially when I listen to Dirtbag and Rat. They sure aren't fans of mine! But when I stay on my medicine, things are all right. When I take my medicine on time, I'm okay.

I wasn't always mixed up like this, though. I can still remember things from when I was younger. My life was great back then. I had a lot of friends. I liked music. I got good grades without even trying. My biggest problem in those days was getting my hair to look right in the mornings, that and having a pimple once in a while. It was nice. . . .

Suddenly there's a loud, roaring sound just outside the coffee shop. It's a huge noise. Frosty, who is standing right next to the doorway that leads out into the front of the coffee shop, peeks around real quick, then turns back toward us.

"What is it?" Stormy asks.

"A fucking tank!" Frosty says, his face red and his hands shaking.

"A what?!" Stormy asks, sounding confused.

Frosty yells, "A goddamned TANK, like if we were terrorists and they needed army shit to take us out!"

Stormy hurries over and peeks out the door, then jumps back. He looks scared, but he says, "It's not really a tank. It doesn't have a big cannon thing on top."

"Fuck!" Frosty snaps. "Okay, it's NOT a tank, but

it sure as shit isn't an RV. It's an armor-plated S.W.A.T. knock-down-the-goddamned-walls machine. They'll kill us all if they drive that thing in here! Oh, man, damn it, if the cops don't kill us, they're gonna throw us in jail forever, for sure. We'll never get out of this now, not with all the shit they have out there—and we can't go to jail—we can't!"

When Frosty says the thing about all of us getting killed, one of the little old ladies sitting here on the floor makes this big snorting sound. I look over at her, and I see she's started to cry. The little girl starts to cry again too, and now the little girl's mom is crying. It's turning into a cryathon back here on the floor of the coffee shop.

Frosty and Stormy's eyes dart back and forth, looking at everybody. I think they're real nervous. I hear the cops, and their big machine roaring; Frosty and Stormy must hear this too. Even I can tell that everything is pretty tense. Tense isn't good—bad things happen when things are too tense.

I try to think of something to say to make things better. "Don't worry," I say to Frosty and Stormy, pointing at the crybabies. "They're just scared, I bet."

"You think?" Stormy says. He's probably being sarcastic. I know people do that, like before, pretend they're asking a question when they're not *really* asking. But sarcasm doesn't work on me 'cause I just don't get it. I've tried really hard to listen for what people call a "sarcastic tone of voice," but I can hardly ever hear it. And I don't know how to be sarcastic myself. This time I figure I should probably answer just in case he means it.

So I say, "Yeah, I think so. I think they're scared, and they're probably sad about having to sit on the floor and not have their coffee. They maybe wish they could have a maple bar, too, since they're just sittin' here having guns pointed at 'em and stuff. Do you wish you had a maple bar?"

Stormy shakes his head. "Are you trying to be funny?"

I answer, "No, I'm not, honest. Sorry, am I being inappropriate?"

Suddenly the fat suit yells at Stormy, "You can't keep us here!"

Stormy lifts his little silver gun up so that's it's pointed right at the fat suit's chest, and then Stormy says to him, "You can try to leave anytime you want."

The fat suit freezes. Neither he nor Stormy moves a muscle. The only sound in the world, other than all the cop noises outside, is the hum of a big freezer or heater or whatever it is that's behind the closed closet door in the back of this little room. Stormy and the fat suit just stare at each other.

Frosty finally steps in and says to the fat suit, "Listen, mister, we don't want to be here any more than you do, but we're all stuck now and that's the way it is." He pauses, then says, "Just cool your jets, big boy. If you tried to leave, they'd just run you over with their tank anyway."

The fat suit looks at their guns. His face, which was bright red a few seconds ago, turns pale. He says, "Okay. Sorry."

Everybody's quiet.

"*Zach, you're a wong-gong.*"

Why doesn't this stuff ever make sense to me?

"'*Cause you're a gong—wong is a gong, gong is a wong.*"

I don't know what that means either.

"*Yes, you do, yes, you do: Wong is a gong, gong is a wong!*"

I hate to admit it, but I guess I do know what a "wong-gong" is, that part is kind of true. I just don't like it.

"YOU NEED TO LET THOSE PEOPLE COME OUT RIGHT NOW."

I wait for wong-gong or gong-wong.

But Frosty moves quickly to the door of the back room and peers out. Frosty yells back, "WE DON'T WANNA HURT ANYBODY. BACK OFF AND GET YOUR TANK OUT OF HERE!"

Wow! Frosty's talking back to the voice; he hears it too.

But after a few seconds I realize that the loud voice is one of the cops yelling at us from outside.

Now the cop yells again, "LET SOME OF THE HOSTAGES GO, AS A SIGN OF GOOD FAITH, AND MAYBE WE'LL GET RID OF THE RESCUE VEHICLE."

Frosty yells back, "THERE AREN'T ANY HOSTAGES. THESE PEOPLE, THEY AREN'T HOSTAGES, AND I'M NOT TALKING TO YOUR ASS UNTIL YOU LOSE THAT *FUCKING* TANK!"

The cop yells back, "OKAY, CALM DOWN— I'LL TALK TO MY PEOPLE OUT HERE. YOU JUST STAY CALM AND DON'T HURT ANYBODY."

"Wing-wong—hostage-gong—wing-wong—wong hostage-dong."

Stormy moves over and stands real close to Frosty, talking in a whisper but loud enough so that I hear. "What're we gonna do?"

Frosty nods toward the old ladies. "Maybe we

should send them out—buy some time until we can figure something out."

Stormy says, "You sure?"

Frosty thinks for a second, then says, "No, I guess not. The cops don't know anything about us, but they will if these ladies go out and tell 'em. It's best if they don't know everything that's happening in here."

One of the old ladies whines, "We won't tell them anything. Please just let us go."

Frosty says to her, "You'll all be fine in a little while, but we gotta get out of this first."

The cop suddenly yells again, "OKAY, WE'RE MOVING THE VEHICLE. WE'RE GOING TO GIVE YOU SOME TIME TO THINK ABOUT IT. YOU THINK ABOUT LETTING SOME OF THOSE FOLKS OUT!"

Suddenly I hear the roaring sound of the cops' tank, or whatever it is. Frosty hurries over to the door and peeks around. "*Adios*," he says as the engine sound grows fainter and farther away.

I say to Stormy, "If we could just get to the maple bars, I bet we'd all feel a lot better."

Stormy shakes his head and says to me, "Are you sure you're not retarded?"

4

Clearwater State Hospital at Greenville,
Dr. Cal Curtis, clinical note based on
observation of Zach's first morning:

When Zach woke up today, the first thing
he appeared to notice was a sparrow on
the brick ledge outside his window. The
medication we gave Zach last night
perhaps helps him to realize that this
sparrow is just a bird, not a "zombie."
Still, Zach's expression remains one of
confusion and fear.

The cops seem kind of quiet now. I guess the police really are giving Frosty some time to think about
things. They say that in movies a lot; I guess they do
it in real life, too.

We are all just sitting here. Nobody says a word.
It reminds me of the first time I was in the hospital.
Everybody just sat around there, too. Dr. Curt said we
were all quiet because we didn't have any "trust" yet.
Maybe everybody's quiet here because we don't have

any trust either. Maybe sitting on the floor, hungry for maple bars while a couple guys wave guns all over the place, makes trust kind of hard.

Okay, maybe if I start, like in group therapy, everybody will start to trust each other—it worked in the hospital.

So I tell Stormy, "Like I told you, I'm not retarded. I just have a brain that works different than other people's brains."

"Right, who cares?" Stormy says, and looks away.

Frosty asks, "Is that why you take medicine?"

I nod.

Stormy is ignoring me, but Frosty is listening, so maybe the trust is working, at least with him. Still, he looks confused. His forehead is all wrinkled, and his eyes look like the eyes of a kid I once saw at a spelling contest who was stuck.

Frosty finally says, "Your parents screwed you up, huh?"

I tell him, "No, my parents, how they raised me and stuff, didn't make me the way I am. You don't get like me by being abused or told you're stupid or having your nose rubbed in your sheets if you pee your bed."

This happened to a depressed guy I met in the hospital. When he was a little kid, his dad actually

27

rubbed his nose on his sheet when the kid wet, like the kid was a dog or something. The kid said it took him weeks to stop smelling the pee smell after his dad did that, but that he still couldn't stop peeing his bed.

I tell Frosty, "You don't get like me from anything that happens when you're growing up. You just get it if it's in your genes."

Stormy laughs and says, "It's in your jeans, all right."

Frosty shakes his head and says, "Bummer."

I notice, again, the gun in Frosty's hand.

Suddenly I start to wonder what it feels like to get shot. I know it sounds stupid that I haven't thought of this before, but lots of times it takes me a while to catch up with stuff.

I wonder if Frosty and Stormy are going to shoot me. Like in that movie *Pulp Fiction*. The bad guys shoot lots people in that movie. I'm definitely *NOT* going to ask them about *Pulp Fiction* or about shooting us. I don't want to give them any bad ideas.

I don't even want to think about getting shot, and so I try to be real quiet.

While I'm being quiet, everybody else is, too—so much for building trust.

After whispering to Stormy, Frosty says, "Okay,

everybody, we've got an announcement."

All of us look at Frosty, but before he can say anything else, I hear words flying out of my mouth. . . .

"Frosty," I ask, "did you ever see that movie *Pulp Fiction*?"

5

Transcript of videotaped recording of
Zach's first meeting with Dr. Curtis at
Clearwater State Hospital at Greenville:

Dr. Curtis: "You know you're here at
Clearwater State Hospital, right?"

Zach nods.

Dr. Curtis (smiling): "This is a safe
place. Our main job here is to make sure
you're safe, okay?"

"Yeah, I saw *Pulp Fiction*." Frosty says.

I ask, "Are you guys gonna shoot us, like they did in that movie?"

Stormy laughs, but it's a mean laugh, and he says; "Just you, pal."

Frosty gives Stormy a shove and quickly says to me, "No, he's just messing with you. We don't wanna shoot anybody if we can help it. But like I was saying before, we've got an announcement, so listen up."

Frosty pauses for a second until we're all looking at him. Even though I usually can't figure out "social cues," I'm guessing, by looking at everybody's faces, that I should stay quiet again.

Frosty says, "We're trying to figure out some way to get out of this mess. We can't think of any way yet. We don't want to hurt any of you, but we're *NOT* gonna go to jail and right now you're the only thing keeping us from that. So we're all gonna have to just sit tight for a while until we figure out how we can work a deal."

The skinny suit, who hasn't said a single word until now, suddenly says, "It's not fair." His voice is real whiny.

Frosty looks at him and says, "No shit, Sherlock, but that's the way it is."

The old lady with the purple-pink hair sitting closest to me, who smells so nice, speaks up. "You're going to have to face the music sometime, you know. That's the way it is too!" She sounds real strict and mean. Her voice is old too; it sounds like a squeaky door.

But she smells so nice. I close my eyes and I breathe in her scent. If I don't look at her, at all her wrinkles and stuff, once she stops talking and I just smell her, I imagine that she's a beautiful girl and that . . .

"*Wong-gong, wong-gong, happy long long dong.*"

"Shut up," I say.

The old lady looks at me now. She looks pissed.

I say to her, "I wasn't talking to you, lady." I don't

Robber-snobber . . .

like her much, even if she does smell nice.

Frosty lifts his hand, the one without a gun, up to his mouth, but I can tell he's grinning. Maybe he doesn't like pissed-off old ladies either.

I hear a real loud crackle sound. It's coming from the cops outside again. A second later there's a voice, and it's got that real scratchy sound of coming through a broken stereo speaker. I can't make out what they're saying, but I hear "hostage situation," "ten-four," "affirmative." It's just like a cops movie. Cops and robbers.

"Robber-snobber . . . wong-gong . . . long-long."

I'm hearing that a lot more now, and that's not good. I wonder when I'm going to get my medicine.

Frosty and Stormy are looking at the door, listening to all the noise coming from out front. Across the room I notice the guy who works here at the coffee shop sneaking toward one of the shelves near where he sits. I look where he's moving and I see what he's doing. On the bottom shelf, under some white tablecloths, is a big knife. I watch the guy slowly reach up toward the handle. . . .

"Get your hand off that!" Stormy yells.

The store guy freezes but looks mad, too. He just stares at Stormy.

Then Stormy says, "I mean it, man. Get your hand

away from that knife."

He shoves his gun right up against the guy's head.

Frosty goes over to them and points *his* gun at the store guy. Frosty says, "What the fuck do you think you're doing?"

With Frosty's gun pointed at the coffee-shop guy, Stormy takes his gun away from the guy's head.

The coffee-shop guy's face is bright red and his lips quiver. He moves his hand off the knife but spits out, "Fuck you."

BLAM!

The sound in this little room is the loudest thing I've ever heard!

That *blam* goes *blam-blam-blam-blam* like an echo through my skull, and then I hear a real high-pitched ringing. The old ladies lift their hands to cover their ears, the fat suit grabs his chest like his heart's gonna explode, the skinny suit begins to shake.

I think, right away, about *Pulp Fiction*! Who's been shot?

Stormy almost drops his gun; he stares at it like it's some weird alien thing.

"Jesus, Joey!" Frosty yells at Stormy.

I think, Who's Joey?

Stormy yells back to Frosty, "I didn't mean it. It just went off."

"Just went off?" Frosty says. "Are you crazy?!"

He looks around at all of us. "Is everybody okay?"

The little girl has wet her pants. Actually her dress. At first I wonder if her mom will rub her nose in the pee, but her mother hugs her close, saying, "It's all right, Katy, you're all right."

"Damn!" Frosty says.

"I didn't mean to," Stormy says again. His voice sounds shaky like he might start crying. He holds the gun down at his side, and his shoulders are droopy.

Frosty says to him, "It's okay, man. Nobody's hurt." He looks around at all of us and asks again, "Nobody's hurt, right?"

Everybody says no except for the mom and the little girl, who don't say anything.

Stormy looks at the little girl who peed her dress, then asks the waitress girl who works at the coffee shop, "Is there a rest room back here?"

The waitress girl grabs a wastebasket next to where she sits and throws up into it.

"Shit!" Frosty says.

The guy who tried to grab the knife puts his arm over the girl's shoulder and yells at Frosty, "Asshole!"

Frosty points his gun at the guy and yells, "Fuck you! You had to go be a big hero!"

Frosty hurries over and grabs the big knife off the shelf and throws it out the doorway, into the main room of the coffee shop.

A phone, sitting on the desk right next to me, rings. I pick it up and say, "Hello?"

Frosty yells at me, "Hang that up!"

The man on the phone yells, "What's happened in there?"

So I answer, "The little girl peed her dress."

"You shot her for that?" the voice yells.

I answer, "No."

"HANG UP!" Frosty yells again

"That was a gunshot, wasn't it?"

"It just went off," I say.

Frosty points his gun at me.

The man on the phone asks, "You shot her by accident?"

"She's not shot."

"We heard a shot!"

Just then I see where the bullet from Stormy's gun went.

"The desk is shot," I say.

"Who?"

"The desk is shot, right through the drawer."

I look at Frosty, and he cocks his gun, pointing it at my head.

"Listen, son," the cop says, sounding calmer. "You need to throw your weapon out and just come out of there before somebody gets hurt. . . ."

"*Wong-gong—gong-wong.*"

Why does he think I have a weapon? How can I throw it out if I don't have it?

"*Throw it out . . . throw up . . . throw rug . . .*"

Frosty's coming toward me.

"Are you still there, son?" the voice asks, interrupting my thoughts.

I say once more, "The desk got shot. . . . I gotta go now."

I hang up the phone.

Frosty stops and stands there staring at me.

I'm wondering whether I should have said "Have a nice day" before I hung up.

But now I notice that everybody is staring, and they are all dead quiet.

"Did you have a nice chat?" Frosty asks.

"I dunno. I was wondering whether I should have said—"

Frosty interrupts, yelling, "Why the fuck did you pick up the phone?"

I say, "It was ringing."

Frosty asks, "Did you really think it was for *you*?"

The second he says this, I remember my mom. I look at my watch. It's three fifty-seven!

"Wow!" I say. "My mom's waiting for me. I need my medicine. I gotta go, now."

I start to stand up, but both Frosty and Stormy jerk up their guns and point them at me.

Frosty says, "You're not going anywhere. What's your name?"

I look at their guns and sit back down. "Zachary McDaniel Wahhsted."

"Zachary," Frosty says.

"Zach," I say. "Not Wasteoid, okay?"

"Okay," Frosty says. "Zach, not Wasteoid . . . you got it. Listen, Zach, if the phone rings again, it's *not* your mom and it's *not* for you, so leave it alone, okay?"

I say, "Sure, Frosty. I'm sorry."

Actually I'm not really sorry, but people usually stop being mad at me whenever I say it.

Frosty says, "Just don't do it again."

Suddenly there's the loud sound of footsteps running on the roof. Everybody in the room looks up, as if we could look through the ceiling.

Stormy says to Frosty, "Cops?"

Frosty answers, "No, Rudolph and Blitzen and Shitzen and Santa, too. Of course cops! Christ!"

The footsteps get louder.

Even though I can see that Frosty doesn't want me to say anything more, I can't stop myself. "The bad guys with guns in that *Pulp Fiction* movie shoot a lot of people."

Frosty is still looking up at the ceiling, but he says, "Yeah, they do, they sure do."

He keeps looking up, but he asks, "Have you ever shot anybody, Zach?"

I shake my head no, but I don't tell him I almost did. Me.

Frosty, still staring at the ceiling, says, "I haven't shot anybody either, Zach." He pauses a second and looks around at all of us sitting here. "But there's always a first time."

6

Clearwater State Hospital—Transcript of
videotaped recording of Zach's second
session with Dr. Curtis:

Dr. Curtis: "When a brain works the way
yours works, Zach, you can't tell what to
feel. If I were to tell you that your mom
is dead and that the candy machine is out
of candy bars, which news would make you
sadder?"

Zach sits very still, glancing around
the office, expressionless and without any
emotion. Finally, after several moments,
Zach responds.

Zach: "Would they put more candy bars
in the machine pretty soon?"

Frosty and Stormy are in the corner, whispering
back and forth again, looking at Stormy's gun and
arguing.

The sound of the cops on the roof is gone now,
but there're still lots of cop sounds outside in the front.

I guess even though they said they'd give Frosty and Stormy time to think, the cops aren't going anywhere.

I feel a little better since Frosty explained about not shooting anybody. Frosty's a nice guy for an armed robber, I guess.

But it's almost four o' clock now—I'm trying hard not to worry about what might happen if I don't take my medicine pretty soon. I'm trying hard not to worry about Dirtbag and Rat showing up either, which sometimes happens when I'm late with my meds. I'm trying not to worry, but *trying* not to worry isn't the same as *not* worrying.

Frosty walks over and picks up the wastebasket that the girl threw up in. "You done with this?" he asks.

The girl nods.

Frosty carries the wastebasket across the room and sets it on the floor in the open doorway. He pushes it so that it slides out into the other room of the coffee shop.

Now he turns around and looks at us. He says, "I'm not sure how in the hell things got so out of control here. None of you are shot yet and none of you will be, but you gotta cooperate. No more hero shit!"

I look around at everyone while Frosty is talking. The guy who tried to grab the knife still looks really mad. The two old ladies just stare at the floor. The girl who got sick isn't looking up either, but she stares off into space, like she's in shock or something. Suddenly I have a terrible feeling about her, she *could* be a zombie—her eyes are red and her skin is white and she stares into space like she's not really here. She could definitely be a zombie, she really could. I'm gonna have to keep my eye on her.

Since Frosty got rid of the wastebasket, it doesn't smell like throw-up in here anymore, which is good because I hate the smell of barf. The two suits look like they've looked the whole time, scared Laurel and Hardy look-alikes. As I look at everybody, I notice that none of them look at me and I wonder if I'm invisible right now. People don't like to look at me, so they pretend I'm invisible. You know, maybe I am?

I jerk my arm up into the air real fast like I'm raising my hand in class, then pull it down just as fast. Everybody looks at me, then looks away, except the skinny suit, who stares at me with a completely grossed-out expression, like he's looking at a worm or toe jam. Then he says, "Jesus," and shakes his head.

The fat suit says, "Just ignore him—he's nutty as a fruitcake."

I ask them, "Do you like maple bars?"

The fat suit says, "Shut up, nut job!"

Frosty says to the man, "*You* shut up."

The fat suit shuts up.

Everybody does. I leave my arm down at my side. I guess I'm not invisible. I guess that's a relief . . . kind of. . . .

Man, I need my medicine. Now I feel the weird feelings, bad feelings under my skin, like ants are crawling over me, or like there's something horrible swimming in my blood.

"*Wong-gong, wong-gong—you're a stupid wong-gong.*"

Maybe I am. . . .

I'm starting to feel worse and worse.

7

Clearwater State Hospital—Transcript of videotaped recording of Zach's second session with Dr. Curtis:

Dr. Curtis (holds a photo album that Zach seems to recognize): "Your mom brought this in. She thought it might help you remember who you are."

They look at the photographs in Zach's family album. After a while, Zach starts to cry. "That's not me," he says, "not anymore."

The phone rings. This time I just leave it alone. Frosty picks it up and says, "Hello."

Frosty is quiet a few moments. Now he yells, "Back off. We're working on it!"

Then he says, "Uh-huh," a couple times, nodding his head.

Now he says, "I'm sixteen, why?"

Frosty listens for a couple seconds, then yells, "Bullshit! You'll try us as adults; I see that shit in the newspaper all the time. Hell, last year you guys wanted to try a *nine-year-old* as an adult! A couple years ago I remember somewhere they *executed* a fifteen-year-old."

Frosty listens again for a while, and now he says, "Oh, you promise, huh? What's that supposed to mean to me? Will you put it in writing?" He hesitates for a few seconds and says, "I'll think about it."

He listens some more. Now he says, "No, really, I mean it, back off and I'll think about it."

Frosty says, "Okay," a few more times. "Yeah, I got it." He hangs up the phone and just stares at the floor.

All of us sit and stare at him. Finally Frosty turns to Stormy and says, "The cops say that they won't charge us with kidnaping if we let everyone go in the next ten minutes. They also say they won't charge us as adults, which means that maybe we won't do jail time, or at least not as much. They say they'll charge us as juveniles."

I blurt out, "Like juvenile delinquents."

Frosty says, "Yeah, Zach, just like juvenile delinquents: real-life, kidnaping, gun-toting, coffee-shop-robbin' J.D.'s. Shut up, okay?"

I say, "Okay."

Stormy says to Frosty, "Ten minutes?"

"Yeah," Frosty answers.

Stormy asks, "And they'll put it in writing?"

"Yep," Frosty says, but then he adds, "Course, we don't know what that means exactly. They could just tear it up once everybody is free and they've got us, right? I mean, if we ask for a lawyer, how do we know they won't just take some cop, hide a gun up his ass, and he'll waltz in here and blow us away? We don't know any lawyers. Johnny Cochran probably isn't available, and Mom sure as hell doesn't know any lawyers."

Stormy says, "Mom? Are the cops gonna tell Mom?"

Frosty sighs and says to Stormy, "Yeah, I'm sure they will once they get us. I mean, come on, think about it."

"I don't want them to tell Mom," Stormy answers. He looks again like he might start to cry, then says, "She'll blame herself."

"Yeah, I know," Frosty says, "but we can't do anything about it now. This whole thing was one dumbass idea."

Stormy says, "She's too sick. . . . she's—"

"Just don't think about it, okay?" Frosty interrupts, "We'll figure it out later. Right now we gotta find some way to get out of this."

Stormy nods, but I think he's still upset, because he keeps staring at the floor and won't look up.

The skinny suit says, "My brother-in-law is a lawyer."

Frosty looks at him and says, "Great, good for him. How's that help us?"

The skinny suit says, "Maybe he'd come down and witness the agreement, you know, make sure the police do what they're supposed to do."

Frosty thinks about this for a few seconds and asks, "What kind of lawyer is he?"

Skinny says, "He does probate and estate planning, you know, so that when you pass away your relatives can inherit your property while minimizing their tax burden and—"

Frosty yells, "We don't need any help making out a damned will, and we're not dead yet, asshole!"

Skinny shuts up.

The phone rings again.

Frosty snatches it up real quick, "Listen, asshole," he yells "we're talking about what to do, we're . . ." He stops suddenly. His face turns real red. "I'm sorry," he says. "No, ma'am." His voice sounds different, quiet now. "No, ma'am, he's fine, honest!

"I'm sorry," he says, then, "Yes, he's right here."

The next thing, Frosty turns to me. He puts his hand over the phone and whispers, "Sorry, Zach." He sounds like he's just had a bad spanking. "It's your mom!"

8

Patient discharge note from Dr. Cal Curtis re: Zachary Wahhsted:

Zach states that the "wong-gong" words are still with him, but that they aren't as loud or frequent as they previously were. He is well medicated and ready for a trial release to his family home (an excellent, caring environment). One concern: Zach states that when he's late with his meds, he feels "weird in every inch" of his body; in schizophrenic adolescent males this kind of sensation is frequently associated with a high suicide risk.

"Hi, Mom," I say, and my mom starts to cry. "Don't cry, Mom. I'm sorry I'm late, but Frosty says I gotta stay."

I say, "I'm sorry" again, because I know that's what normal people say when somebody is crying and because saying it always makes my mom feel better.

"Are you okay, honey?" Mom asks. She's stopped crying, so the "I'm sorry" worked.

wing-wong

"Yes," I answer. "But I'm kinda hungry."

"Okay, honey," Mom says. Then she asks, "Zach, are you hurt at all?"

I think about it. "My butt's kinda sore," I say.

Mom asks real quick, "What did they do to you, Zach?"

"The floor is hard and kinda cold."

"Oh," Mom says, and asks, "Are the guys who are holding you being mean?"

"No," I say, although I'm not sure exactly if that's true or not. I mean, having the guns pointed at us is kind of mean, I suppose. But Frosty hasn't called me Wasteoid once, and Stormy just seems to do what Frosty says. So I don't know for sure.

Mom says, "I've gotta go, honey. The police need the phone. But I'm waiting here for you, okay? The police can't let me come in, but I'm waiting right here, Zach, okay?"

"Okay, Mom," I say.

Mom asks, "Is there anything else you need? Is there anything we can get for you?"

I think about it for just a second. I look at the zombie girl again. She makes me nervous. "Yeah," I answer, "I need my medicine."

Mom says, "I know, honey, I know. The police can't let me come in, but I have it right here."

9

Letter from Dr. Calvin Curtis to Ms. Emily Wahhsted, mother of Zachary Wahhsted:

Many times patients like Zach believe that it is the medication that makes them feel poorly. They lower their dosage without telling us. At first things sometimes do seem better. Patients often believe that maybe they will be all right without their medicine. This is an *extremely* dangerous misperception. . . .

After I hang up, I think more about my medicine. I'm really worrying that Dirtbag and Rat might show up soon. But maybe they can't get through the cops—maybe. I hate it when they come—it's the worst. Lots of times I'm a little late with my meds and nothing bad happens, but when I'm under stress . . . well, sometimes . . . I don't even want to think about it. . . .

"Listen up," Frosty says. "I want to let you guys outa here. This wasn't supposed to go down like this, and this offer from the cops sounds like our best chance. But I don't trust the police. We have our reasons for

long-long

doing this, and they're important, so don't think we won't do what we have to. But if there's some way we can get you guys out of here without screwing us up, we'll do it."

The nice-smelling old lady sitting next to me says, "You might think you have a good reason, but it's still wrong!" Her words sound even meaner than before.

Frosty looks at her and quietly says, "You wouldn't understand, lady."

But the old lady keeps talking. "Whatever's wrong in your lives, do you think it will help anything for you to go to jail? You think it will help anything if the police gun you down like a couple of dogs?" Her voice is like she's swearing even though her words aren't swear words.

The other old lady touches her friend's arm and says, "Ethel, please."

The mean lady says, "Well, they deserve whatever happens to them. They're punks!"

The nicer lady says, "They're just boys whose mother is ill. . . ."

Stormy asks, "How'd you know that?"

The nice old lady looks up at him and says, "I heard you mention something about it. That's right, isn't it? Are you boys doing this to try and help your mother?"

Stormy starts to answer, "Yes, ma'am. We need money to—"

Frosty interrupts Stormy. "Shut up," he says. "Listen, lady, no offense, but it's a private family matter."

The nice lady looks at Frosty and nods. She turns to her mean friend and says softly, "They're just boys, Ethel."

Frosty looks at the ladies and takes a deep breath. He doesn't say anything. He looks pissed. Why did that old lady have to say the thing about them being gunned down? I don't think that helped.

Stormy asks Frosty, "We gonna let them go?"

Frosty nods. "I guess so. We're gonna have to do something, or the cops are gonna bust in here sooner or later."

"What if the cops are lying about everything?"

Frosty answers, "We'll have to take our chances."

Stormy yells, "No! If we let everybody go, they'll just come in and shoot us, won't they? That's what's gonna happen. We're gonna be dead—Mom's gonna have nobody! Great idea you had here, genius."

Frosty screams, "Shut up, Joey. I'm gonna figure something out, but we gotta let these people go or it'll be worse. Just stop bitching."

As Frosty talks, his voice gets higher and higher, and for the first time since they came in, he sounds like *he* might start crying.

Frosty yells, "Maybe we should just shoot everybody and then kill ourselves! What's the point of anything, what's the difference?" He's waving his gun around while he's yelling.

Everybody's quiet. The store guy still has his arm around the girl's shoulders (if he's not careful, she could turn him into a zombie, too). Nobody takes a breath.

Frosty finally says, "We'll let everyone go but one person. Somebody's gotta stay and—"

Fat suit interrupts. "Keep the loony"—looking over at me.

Without planning it out or thinking it through, I say, "Sure, I'll stay with you guys. . . ." Frosty and Stormy just look at me like they don't understand, so I explain, "If you're worried about being in here by yourselves, I'll stay."

Frosty says, "Jesus Christ, Zach, that's all we need, to be stuck in here with *you* for the rest of our lives."

The fat suit lets out a loud laugh, but when he does, Frosty glares at him and the fat suit stops laughing right away.

Frosty turns to me and says, "I don't really know if it would even help for you to stay here, Zach."

I don't know either, but they look really scared. I remember what being scared used to feel like, so I say, "If you'd let me call Dr. Curt, he'll make the police let me have my medicine—then I can stay. If I don't get my medicine pretty soon, Dirtbag and Rat will come—"

Frosty looks confused. "Who the hell are they? Friends of yours?"

I answer, "No, no way. But listen, Dr. Curt—"

Frosty interrupts me again, "Who's this Dr. Curt guy?"

"He's my doctor," I say.

Frosty asks, "Do you trust him?"

I do trust him, he's my friend, so I answer, "Yeah, he helps me."

Frosty asks, "Do you think he'd help us, too?"

I ask, "Do you need medicine?"

Stormy mumbles, "What a moron!" He says to Frosty, "You can't trust this idiot!"

Ignoring Stormy, Frosty says, "No, Zach, we don't need medicine, but do you think your doctor would talk to the cops? Doctors take oaths to help people, right? Do you think that maybe he'd look at what they write and help us get out of here?"

I don't understand Frosty's question. But I think zombie girl has a new friend. Skinny suit just keeps staring at the floor like a zombie now too. I need to talk to Dr. Curt and I need my medicine now! The only thing I can think to answer Frosty is, "All I can tell you is that Dr. Curt always helps me."

Frosty thinks for a second, then shrugs and says, "That's good enough for me. Let's call him up."

10

*Letter from Ms. Emily Wahhsted to Dr. Cal
Curtis:*

. . . Thanks for your concerns. Zach
seemed to have a good first week. But now,
after two weeks, he says there are two
"new" "meaner" voices bothering him. What
does this mean? As you suspected, Zach may
not be taking his medicine properly. I found
several pills in his wastebasket. . . .

Dr. Curtis picks up his phone after the second ring.
"Cal Curtis," he answers.

I say, "Hi, Dr. Curt, it's Zach."

"Hi, Zach, how are you?" he asks.

"I'm good," I say.

"Everything's going all right?" he asks. "Your mom's
okay?"

"Oh, yes," I say. It occurs to me that I should say
"thanks for asking," that's what a normal person would
say. So I say, "Thanks for asking."

I should explain to Dr. Curt why I'm phoning, but

55

you're a gong

I can't think how to start. Finally I say, "I'm glad you were at your phone. At your office and stuff, I mean."

Dr. Curt says, "Yes, it's nice to hear from you again too, Zach. But I've got a patient coming in just a few minutes, so I don't have much time to talk right now."

"Okay," I say. "Well, it's been nice talking to you—"

I'm about to hang up the phone when Frosty grabs it from me and says, "Hello!"

He says into the phone, "My name is Alan Mender, and Zach is here with my brother Joey and me. He said we could trust you. We're in a hell of a lot of trouble!"

Aha! Now I know their real names, Alan and Joey. I liked Frosty and Stormy better.

There's a pause, a long one. Dr. Curt is saying something to Frosty—I mean, Alan.

Finally Alan says, "Yes, Dr. Curtis, I know your first concern is Zach. I'll put him on the line, but listen to him, okay?"

He hands the phone to me. "Tell him what's going on here, Zach."

I take the phone and try to think of the words. Before I can say anything, Dr. Curt asks, "Are you all right, Zach? What's going on there, and who is that? He sounds pretty shaky."

I say, "He's real, Dr. Curt."

"I know, Zach, yes, he's real."

I still can't even think how to start, so I just say the things that are in my brain. "I guess his real name's Alan. . . ."

I think, I wish his name was Frosty. . . . It's such a cool name. I wish his name was Frosty and *mine* was Stormy, not Wasteoid. . . . I wish . . .

"Okay, Zach, it's okay," Dr. Curt says. "Can you explain what's happening?"

Now the words just tumble out of my mouth. "He has a gun and it's real. His brother Joey has one, too, and he shot the drawer and the little girl peed her pants—I mean her dress. I can't go get my medicine or any maple bars because the police would shoot us, but there's two guns and two brothers and everybody gets to leave if you'll come here and bring my medicine, 'cause I'm gonna stay till you help us, okay?"

Dr. Curt says, "You bet, Zach." He pauses a second, then asks, "Can I speak to Alan? The boy I spoke to a few moments ago, can I speak to him again?"

I say, "Sure," and I wait for Dr. Curt to say something more.

Dr. Curt finally asks, "Zach, would you give Alan the phone *now*, please?"

I say, "Oh, yeah, sure." I turn to Alan. "He wants to talk to you again."

Alan takes the phone and listens for a few moments,

then says, "I don't want to use the word hostages, but yeah, nine counting Zach." Alan pauses for a few seconds, listening to Dr. Curt. Now Alan explains about the police and the old ladies and the suits and everything else.

Alan finally says, "The cops say they'll put a deal in writing, but we don't know if we can trust them. This Zach kid"—Alan looks at me—"he says you can help us, mister. To be honest, we're pretty scared and right now we just wanna get out of as much trouble as we can. Zach says we can trust you. I don't think Zach lies much, you know? I don't think he knows how. So can you help us?"

Alan listens for a few seconds, then says, "Thank you, sir, thank you so much. One more thing, will you call our mom, Louise Mender, before the cops find out who we are? They'll scare her. We don't want her to see this on the news."

Alan listens some more, then tells Dr. Curt his mom's phone number, then says, "Okay, Dr. Curt . . . thanks."

Alan hangs up the phone and turns to me. "Okay, he's coming here and he's bringing your medicine. Are you really willing to wait here with us until he gets here?"

"Sure," I say.

Alan looks at me kind of funny and asks, "Aren't you scared, man? Aren't you at least a little bit afraid of dying?"

I tell him the truth, "No," but I don't tell him the whole truth, that dying, for a long time now, has been the least of my worries.

Alan takes a deep breath and pauses, looking around at everyone.

Even though Alan's seen *Pulp Fiction*, I don't think he's looking at us like he wants to shoot us. . . . Then again, how would I know for sure?

11

Letter from Ms. Emily Wahhsted to Dr. Cal Curtis:

Zach told me that a new voice constantly calls him "worthless," a "worthless wasteoid." Zach says that he tries to ignore this, but that when he does, another new voice, the second one, screams at him. I don't know how to answer when Zach asks me why they hate him so much, when he asks what he ever did to them to deserve this. What he ever did to anyone.

Alan picks up the phone and dials the number the cops gave him and says, "We're going to send everyone out but Zach, the kid whose mom called before. He's gonna stay with us until we see the deal in writing from you and his shrink gets here and tells us that it looks all right."

Alan pauses and listens, then says, "No, he is *not* being kept against his will. He agreed to stay, free and clear." Alan listens some more and turns to me. He covers the mouthpiece of the phone and says, "Damn it, the cop wants to talk to you."

I say, "Okay."

I take the phone from Alan. His hand shakes as he hands it to me.

I say, "Hello."

The voice says, "You need to come out of there, son."

"You think so?"

"Yes, otherwise you're in real danger. Not to mention, by not leaving, you could be aiding and abetting in the commission of a felony."

"I don't know what abetting means."

"You know right from wrong, don't you?" the cop asks, sounding kind of mad.

The truth is the whole right-from-wrong thing *is* a little confusing to me at times. "Maybe not," I answer.

"Don't get smart with me, son."

"*Wing-wong, wing-wong, wing-wong smart smarty—dumb dong.*"

The cop says, "If you stay in there of your own free will, we can't promise that you won't get hurt."

"Do you like maple bars?" I ask.

"Jesus!" the cop snaps.

how stupid you are

Suddenly I hear my mom's voice in the background. I can't hear all she says, but some parts of it come over the line, including, ". . . talk to my son that way . . . Yell at *my* boy . . ." and now Mom says some swear words, too.

I hear the cop speaking back to Mom like he's sorry, which I bet he is—it's not a good idea to get my mom pissed at you for being mean to me. Dr. Curt once said, "Your mom's a butt kicker and a name taker when it comes to protecting you, Zach. You're lucky to have her!"

The cop says to me, "Listen, Zachary, I'm sorry I yelled at you and—"

I interrupt him, "That's okay, but I'm tired of talking." My skin is starting to feel like ants are crawling all over me again, and zombie girl and the skinny suit are both staring at me. I say, "Thanks for calling. Have a nice day. 'Bye." I hang up.

Alan says, "That was easy."

I ask, "It was? If you say so. Hey, do you see ants crawling on me?"

Alan shakes his head and looks down. I think I make him uncomfortable. I do that to people.

Suddenly the zombie girl says to me, "There aren't any ants on you."

I'm afraid to look at her again, but finally I do. She looks normal now—maybe she's okay. But zombies can be tricky. I'm still going to keep my eye on her.

"Go ahead, Wasteoid, show them how stupid you are."

I put my hands up over my ears and the voice stops for now. But I need my meds. I need them bad!

Alan looks around the room at everybody and says, "We're gonna let you go in a minute or two, so don't try anything stupid, okay? It'd be kind of a shame to have to shoot all of you now."

Alan pauses a second; he turns to me. "You too, Zach."

12

Letter from Ms. Emily Wahhsted to Dr. Cal Curtis:

Zach says that he's tried to ignore
the terrible new voices, but that after
listening to them for weeks on end,
death feels like his only escape. He told
me death feels like a good idea.

    Yesterday, Zach came home from school
before I got back from shopping. . . .

Except for Alan and Joey and me, all the other people here in the back of the coffee shop are ready to leave. As soon as the two old ladies stand up, they straighten their clothes, like they planned it out together ahead of time. The fat suit's shirt has stretched really wide across his big belly, and the button just below his tie has come undone. I say to him, pointing at it, "Your button's undone there."

"Oh," he says, and quickly buttons up. "Thanks," he mumbles.

He hasn't looked at me hardly at all. I look

around at everyone else as they stand up. Maybe this sounds bad, but I don't care about any of them. They're strangers, and they're just like everyone else I ever meet, as much like zombies as humans. I glance again at the store girl and skinny suit real fast when I think this; I wonder if they can read my mind. Most people remind me of characters in a cartoon—zombie characters. I know that most other people aren't like me. I think it's why they don't like me much.

The lady with the little girl steps over to where I'm standing and looks at me. "Thank you so much," she says softly, "for helping us."

I say, "You're welcome," even though I don't really know what she means.

"If it weren't for you staying here, I'm not sure they would let us go. . . . I'm not sure what might have happened if it weren't for you. . . ." She starts to cry.

I don't know what to do, so I say, "I'm sorry," the fixer-upper words.

"Pardon me?" she asks softly.

"I'm sorry you're sad." But as I'm saying this, I blurt out, "You're pretty." The second I say it, I know I'm being "inappropriate." But she *is* very pretty; her eyes look friendly, like a dog's eyes. I say to the lady, again, "You're pretty." I also say, just to try and explain

time . . . grime

what I mean, "You have nice dog eyes." This sounds goofy even to me.

"*Wong-dong, ha-ha, long dong long dong long dong.*"

The voice is making fun of me for liking this grown-up lady and for calling her a pretty dog-eyed person. It's also talking about my dong and I feel my face get red.

So I say, "I don't mean that in a bad way."

She smiles at me and touches my arm and says "thank you" again.

"Okay," I say, but when she touches me, I think about her hugging her daughter after the little girl peed, and I can't help but wonder if the lady's hand has pee on it.

While I'm thinking this, the lady hugs her little girl close to her again. I know this pretty mom wouldn't rub her little girl's nose in the sheets if the little girl wet the bed. I'll bet this mom would just give her little daughter a maple bar or something. Life is so weird. One kid gets a nose full of pee, another kid gets loved to bits. Heck, I don't even care if this lady has pee on her hand or not. Life is too weird to worry about a little pee here and there.

• • •

Alan picks up the phone and says, "Everyone but Zach is coming out now." He hangs up.

Alan turns to everyone and says, "Okay, you guys, get outa here!"

Alan and Joey and I peek out the door of the back room as everyone walks away from us. I can't believe that it's dark out now—when we came into this room, it was daytime, but now it's night already. Sometimes it's hard for me to keep track of time—to be honest, time doesn't make sense to me anymore.

"Time . . . grime . . . pantomime . . . long-gone wong-gong is a wong-gone long gong . . ."

The itching on my skin is getting worse—I feel hot now, too.

The others move slowly toward the door. The police shine bright lights through the windows—they're kind of blue. All the people look blue, which makes them *all* look like zombies. I know they're not really zombies, even the store girl or skinny suit, at least I don't think so—but I'm not sure anymore.

Why is everybody moving so slowly? Why don't they just walk out? Then maybe the blue zombie light will shut off. I'd like that.

"WHEN YOU GET TO THE DOOR, STEP

OUT VERY SLOWLY, ONE AT A TIME. PUT YOUR HANDS BEHIND YOUR HEADS AND WALK DIRECTLY TO THE POLICEMAN WAITING FOR YOU."

The skinny suit goes out first. He puts his hands up behind his head, just like he's supposed to, and disappears into the blue light. Next the fat suit leaves, now the old ladies, now the store guy and girl. As everyone goes through the door and walks out, it's pretty quiet. Nobody says anything, and the only sounds are the sounds of the police moving around. Finally the mom and her daughter go out together; the mom holds the little girl close to her side until they reach the door. Now the little girl puts her hands up behind her head just like her pretty mom. Weird. Do the cops think the little girl with the wet spot on her dress is some kind of kidnaping midget terrorist or something? I laugh out loud at this thought. Joey gives me a dirty look.

The bright lights glaring through the windows make it hard to see what happens to everybody once they're out of the coffee shop. For all I know they could be out there shaking hands with the president of the United States—except he's not here, he's probably in Washington, D.C., keeping the world safe for

democracy and stuff. One thing's for sure, though—
all this action, all this fuss, and still no maple bars. I
think the least that should happen is that I get a maple
bar.

Why did I stay here?

13

Letter from Ms. Emily Wahhsted to Dr. Cal Curtis:

Zach says that the two new voices kept torturing him, begging him to kill himself, so he went to my bedroom closet and found the rifle I kept for our "protection." . . .

To be honest, I'm glad everybody except Alan and Joey and I are gone. Most of the time, like I've said, I'm not that thrilled to be around people, 'cause they usually just confuse me. I always feel more relaxed when I'm alone, except for the times when I'm alone for too long and Dirtbag and Rat come after me.

Now that it's just Alan and Joey and me, and since I'm sitting up in a chair instead of on the floor, I feel a lot better. It also feels like there's a ton of room back here now, with all the others gone. I feel pretty happy, actually, even without a maple bar.

It's nice to feel happy and to know I'm feeling it. Does that make any sense? I just mean it's so unusual that I "feel" anything. This is pretty much the way it goes for people with my kind of brain. We just don't feel things. . . . It's hard to explain.

Alan interrupts my thoughts. "So, Zach, this Curtis guy's your doctor? Why is your brain so messed up?" He hesitates a second, then says, "Sorry, I didn't mean it like that, I didn't mean it like . . . never mind."

I ask him, "Why'd you guys do this robbery? Why'd you need money so bad?"

Alan looks at me a second before he answers. "Our mom has cancer. We don't have any medical insurance because Mom had to quit her job. She's really sick from the chemotherapy and radiation treatments, and her medicine costs a fortune. We're down to nothing. We had to get some money, so I came up with this idiotic idea."

"Where's your dad?" I ask. "Dads sometimes help with money."

Joey says, "We don't even know if Dad's alive."

Alan interrupts, yelling, "Fuck you, Joey! He's alive!" But then Alan says, "We just don't know where he is."

I say, "My dad left too, a long time ago." But the truth is I don't even remember him and I don't ever think about him.

long gone . . . like you

"Long gone . . . like you . . . boo-hoo . . . long gone."

Alan pauses a few seconds and stares at me. "I'm sorry you got caught up in this, and I'm sorry if we scared you and kept you here. But the truth is we'd do *anything* to help our mom."

I try to understand, and I say, "I know what you mean. My mom makes meals for me and cleans all my clothes and picks me up after school and gives me my medicine." I try to think of some other reasons to care about my mom. All I can come up with is, "She used to hide Easter eggs for me when I was little. I like eggs." I try to think of *anything* else, *anything* more that I can figure for why I'm glad my mom is around, but finally I give up.

Joey says, "Our mom used to do that kind of stuff for us, too."

Alan looks at him and says, "When Mom gets well, she'll do those things again, Joey."

Joey looks at the floor and nods his head. "Yeah, sure," he says, so softly I can barely hear him.

I ask, "Is your mom gonna die?" The second I ask this, I wonder if it's "appropriate."

Joey gives me a mean look, but Alan answers, "No. I hope not. We don't know for sure, but I don't think she will."

Joey stares back at the floor. He doesn't look at either of us, but he says, "If prayers ever come true, Mom won't die. If there really is a God and if he gives a . . ." He doesn't finish his thought.

Alan asks me, "So this brain thing you've got, when did you know you had it?"

I try to explain. "When I was fourteen, I started to hear voices and got all confused and had to go to the hospital—they said I have schizophrenia."

Alan asks, "So that's when you knew you were messed up, huh? I mean, that's when you knew you were sick?"

I think about it. "No, not really at first, I didn't know *for sure* then. I mean, I knew something was wrong, but I didn't know how bad it would get until I—"

CRASH!

My words are cut off by a loud sound from outside the coffee shop. It's a big crashing sound, like the cops are breaking down the door or kicking in the glass.

Alan and Joey both jump up and pull out their guns real fast. Alan moves over to the door so he can look out.

Joey yells to Alan, "Are they coming?"

Alan yells back, "I don't know!" He turns to me and says, "Get over in that closet, Zach; stay out of the way."

I say, "I won't get in your way."

"Go!" Alan yells. "I don't want you to get hurt."

I go across the room up to the closet door and pull it open. It's kind of dark in there, but it's not really a closet. Through the dark, I see a freezer and some shelves. There's also a door that leads outside. I glance back over my shoulder.

Alan is peeking out at the cops. In the instant he starts to pull his head back, there's another huge noise, the loud, cracking sound of a gunshot.

Alan falls from the doorway and down onto his knees, dropping his gun, which slides across the slick linoleum floor and ends up right at my feet. Joey screams, no words, just a scream. Alan lifts his hands to his face. I pick up the gun. It's real heavy. It seems to be alive, like it's breathing. I know guns aren't alive, but it feels like it is.

I hold the gun carefully and look back at Alan again. He is kneeling on the floor holding his face. I see blood on his fingers.

14

Letter from Ms. Emily Wahhsted to Dr. Cal Curtis:

Zach says he took the rifle and went out and sat on a deck chair. As he sat there, he says, he wondered what I might think when I came home and found his body. I guess some tiny part of him realized that I "might be upset."

The blood on Alan's face looks kinda like chocolate sauce, the kind you put on ice cream. I wish I had a chocolate sundae right now.

The phone rings.

A loud voice booms from outside:

"ARE YOU ALL RIGHT IN THERE? IS EVERYONE ALL RIGHT? THAT WAS A MISTAKE! PICK UP THE PHONE!"

The phone keeps ringing.

Joey just stands frozen, staring at Alan, so I grab the phone.

A voice asks, "Is everybody okay?" He sounds scared.

shoot . . .

I say, "Alan's holding his head—he's bloody!"

"Oh, God," the voice says back.

Alan stands up, brushing off the side of his face. Little pieces of wood fall away. The bullet shattered the wall right next to where Alan's head was. Splinters are sticking into his face, making bloody spots.

I say into the phone, "Alan's face is bleeding."

"Is he conscious? Is he alive?"

Alan walks over to me and grabs the phone out of my hand.

"WHAT THE HELL WAS THAT?" he yells into the phone.

He listens for a second, then yells again. "MISTAKE MY ASS! YOU TRIED TO BLOW MY HEAD OFF!"

Alan listens again, then says, "No," still sounding mad. "I'm okay, but . . ."

Alan listens some more. He says, quieter, "No, it's just a scratch, not that you give a shit."

Alan slams the phone down.

He turns to Joey and me and says, "Accidental shot."

Joey yells, "Accidental? Bull! It only missed your head by about an inch!" As Joey says this, he walks back and forth across the room like I've seen people do in the hospital, pacing like crazy. It's like Joey's ready to kill somebody himself.

Alan says to Joey, "Calm down—the guy wasn't supposed to shoot. He didn't have orders."

Joey says, "I don't believe it. I think they wanna kill us to protect Zach."

Alan says, "Maybe. I don't know what to think anymore."

Suddenly Alan looks at me and notices, for the first time, that I'm holding his gun. Joey notices, too, and snaps his gun up, pointing it right at me. Without even thinking about it, I point Alan's gun at Joey. We stand real still. I look down the barrel of Joey's little gun.

"*Long gong . . . barrel . . . cracker barrel . . . barrel o' monkeys . . . wong-gong.*

"*Shoot . . . shoot. . . . Even better . . . let him shoot you!*"

This isn't good.

Even I can tell this isn't good.

15

Letter from Ms. Emily Wahhsted to Dr. Cal Curtis:

Zach says he came back into the house, got a piece of paper and a pencil, and wrote a note, leaving it for me on the kitchen counter. Then he went back out to the deck and sat back down and picked up the rifle. Can you imagine?

Alan snaps at Joey, "What the hell are you doing? Lower your gun!"

Joey looks at Alan so angrily that not even I can miss it. Joey spins around and punches the wall, but he points his gun at the floor. I point my gun at the floor too.

Alan looks at me. "Hey, Zach, I better have my gun back, okay?"

I look at the gun in my hand and don't say anything for a second.

I look up again at Alan, and he is smiling. He says, "You wanna shoot it?"

Joey paces back and forth again.

I answer Alan about shooting the gun. "I better not."

Alan says, "It's okay—go ahead and pull the trigger if you want to."

I point the gun at Alan, and I ask, "Really? How come? You want to die?" Maybe I'm not the only one who feels that way.

Alan says, "Sure, just pull the trigger."

Joey says, "Wait a sec—"

Alan interrupts him. "It's okay, Joey."

"Fine, whatever!" Joey yells.

I say, "I don't really want to shoot you, Frosty . . . I mean Alan."

Alan says, "Shoot the floor, then."

I say, "Okay."

I point the gun at the floor. I slowly squeeze the trigger. I hear a *click* and nothing more, just a little *click*. I pull the trigger a second time, *click*, a third time, *click*, then a bunch of times, *click*, *click*, *click*, *click*.

Alan reaches over and takes the gun. He looks at it, then says to me, "It doesn't work, hasn't for a long time. It's a World War Two officer's sidearm, a forty-five caliber. Our grandpa was a fighter pilot. All of them carried these, but Grandpa removed the firing pin from this one fifty years ago. Some holdup, huh?"

barrel o' monkeys

16

Letter from Ms. Emily Wahhsted to Dr. Cal Curtis:

Zach, my son, felt horrible enough to put the barrel of the rifle into his mouth.

I'm confused, so I ask, "What about Joey's gun? It works." I look at Joey's gun. "He shot the desk."

When I say this, Joey says, "Yeah, I did, and don't forget it! Don't get any smart ideas—uh-oh, I forgot, you *never* get those."

"Shut up, Joey," Alan says, then looks at me again. "I emptied the bullet clip from Joey's gun, but I forgot to check the chamber and make sure that it was empty, too—"

Joey interrupts him. "Alan, what're you doing?"

"It's okay, Joey," Alan says. He turns to me. "When Joey's gun went off, I almost had a heart attack!"

I ask, "How were you going to shoot us if you don't have guns that work?"

Alan looks at me for a second like he feels sorry for me, but he says, "That's the whole point, Zach—we were never going to shoot anybody. We just wanted to scare everybody until we could get the money, then leave."

I glance around the room where the three of us are sitting. I look at Joey's silver gun and Alan's black one, both useless. I hear the hum from behind the closed closet door. The walls are clean, painted white. I can smell coffee. I look at the doorway, which leads out into the front of the coffee shop.

All of a sudden I realize I could jump up and go running out of here and tell the cops that these two juvenile delinquents, Alan and Joey, can't do diddly-squat 'cause their guns don't even work.

I guess turning in Alan and Joey would be the "appropriate" thing to do. After all, they *are* doing a crime. A "good citizen" would probably turn them in, and if I did, everyone would probably think I'm a hero. It's probably inappropriate of me *not* to do it.

But here's the deal. These two kids aren't so different from me. I mean, I'm sick and messed up and they're messed up now, too. They're probably going to jail, which can't be that different from going to the hospital—all three of us are kind of the same. Plus, neither Alan nor Joey has called me Wasteoid.

I don't know for sure what to think; I mean, after

wing-wong

all, I'm not the best guy to figure out the right thing to do. Heck, I know I'm weird, maybe even crazy! I think about maple bars when I should be worried about getting shot in the head. I think about candy bars when I should be worried about my mom being dead. I think about the color of the walls and the sound of the freezer when I'm surrounded by cops who could shoot me by accident. I know I'm nuts. But I know another thing, too, and I know it for sure—whether a guy is crazy or not, if he gives his word, if he says he's gonna do something, he should stick to it, otherwise he really is a wasteoid. A lot of times my brain makes it hard for me to control what I say or think or do, but I promised Alan and Joey that I'd stay here until Dr. Curt comes and helps. I'm NOT a wasteoid! I'm NOT! I'm going to try my hardest to do what's right. Then I'm going to get my medicine and go home with my mom.

17

Letter from Ms. Emily Wahhsted to Dr. Cal Curtis:

This was the moment I got home, walking into the house and through the kitchen. I saw Zach on the deck, the barrel of the rifle in his mouth. He looked so relaxed, almost happy. I called out to him, and he actually smiled at me.

Alan and Joey talk softly together. I can't really hear what they're saying, but after a little while Joey starts to cry. I don't know what exactly is making him cry right now.

I know people usually feel sorry for somebody who's crying, but I don't feel sorry for him. I don't mean that to sound bad; I don't want people to hate me, but I don't feel anything much for people —that's just the way my brain *doesn't* work. So now I just sit here and watch the tears rolling down Joey's face and the snot dripping out of his nose. I may not feel anything, but I know what I should do. I should help them like I

Time to die!!

promised, so I just sit still and keep the news about their guns not working to myself. When Dr. Curt comes, everything will be okay.

Alan puts his arm around his brother and says, "I'm sorry I got you into this, Joey."

Now Alan starts to cry, too.

I watch them both.

But now the weirdest thing happens. Suddenly I notice a tear running out of the corner of my eye and down my cheek. I put my finger up and touch the tear. I put the tear into my mouth and taste it. It's salty. Wow. Maybe I *do* feel sad for them. Maybe I'm crying because I feel sad. Maybe I'm not so crazy after all! Maybe I'm getting better!

Alan turns to me and says, "Are you okay, Zach?"

"Huh?" I ask. I'm still thinking about the tear. "Yeah, sure, I guess."

Suddenly I remember what Alan and I were talking about earlier, before Alan's face almost got shot. I remember Alan's question about when I first knew I was sick. I never answered him.

I say, "I'm okay, Alan. And I remember when I first knew I was sick, too."

For a second, Alan looks like he doesn't know what I'm talking about, but now I can see by his expression that he remembers. He asks, "Oh, yeah, when did you know?"

"After . . ." I say.

"After?" Alan asks. "After what?"

I pause a second. "After I tried to kill myself. After that I *knew* I was sick. I'm really hungry, Alan. Can't we go get a maple bar from out front?"

18

Letter from Ms. Emily Wahhsted to Dr. Cal Curtis:

Zach just said, "I'm gonna shoot myself, Mom," but before he could get his mouth back down to the gun, I took the rifle away.

"But Mom," Zach said again, "I'm gonna shoot myself."

"Not today, honey," I said, and then I burst into tears.

Alan and Joey both stare at me. People get real quiet when they hear about suicide. Maybe Alan and Joey are freaked out.

Alan asks, "You really tried to kill yourself?"

"Yeah," I answer.

Joey says, "*You* tried to kill yourself? What'd you do, screw that up too?"

Alan gives Joey a shove. "Shut up, asshole!"

I say, "I did try, Joey, really. I was gonna shoot myself, but my mom got home and wouldn't let me."

Joey laughs and says, "What'd you do, ask her permission?"

I answer, "No, she just got home."

Alan shakes his head. I know lots of times people don't say what they're thinking. But Alan's face looks so sad, even I can tell that he feels bad for me, like my mom did when she saw me with the gun that day.

"Christ, Zach," Alan says, his voice kind of shaky, "why'd you wanna do that?" He stops. "I mean . . . how bad can it be?"

I don't know what to say.

Joey is quiet too.

I finally say, mostly just because I think I should say *something*, "It's okay, Alan, don't worry."

Alan says, "I'm sorry, Zach. I guess you got it pretty bad, man. Are you ever going to get better?"

I remember what Dr. Curt has told me about my brain and my illness. I answer Alan truthfully. "No, probably not, but it's okay, Alan."

I wish I could explain to Alan and Joey about going to the hospital that afternoon after I tried to kill myself. I can't find the right words, but I still remember it. It seemed like a long ride back to Clearwater. Mom drove us down Highway 195 southbound, driving fast. I kept thinking that if I just opened the door of the car and dove out onto my head, I'd die for sure; then everything would just be over, no more Dirtbag and Rat, no more confusion, no more—anything. I watched the pavement race by, staring at the white lane-bump markers as they flickered past. After a while, I realized that I hadn't heard the new voices since I'd started to pull the trigger—it was like Dirtbag and Rat knew that if I died, they wouldn't get to torture me anymore. I smiled at that thought, and right then Mom happened to look over at me.

"You okay, Zach?"

"I don't know."

"Are the voices bothering you?"

"No. I'm just thinking about the white dots and dying."

Mom said, "I know, honey. Dr. Curtis is going to talk to us about all this, okay? He's going to help us."

"Okay," I said.

I didn't even feel sad or upset that I hadn't been able to kill myself right; it didn't even matter to me. Neither of us said anything else all the rest of the way to Clearwater.

I won't tell Alan and Joey any more about it, though. Alan seems bummed enough as it is. He looks like he's about ready to kill *himself* just thinking how bad it would be to be me.

Alan says, "I'm sorry, Zach. Sorry you're so screwed up. You're a nice guy—it's too bad." He says this without looking at me, staring at the ground. Joey stares at the ground too. I think he'd almost like to say something, but he can't. I know it's hard for Joey to say anything nice to me; he reminds me of kids from school, who are scared to treat me different than their friends treat me, so they're mean. I never know what to say to those kids. I don't know what to say to Joey either.

I finally say to Alan, "I'm not messed up like that anymore, Alan." I pause and think about it. "At least, I don't want to kill myself today; I don't want to die right now."

Alan says, "That's good, Zach. You're doin' better now, huh?"

Joey interrupts. "Everybody dies someday—most people whether they want to or not, you know? At least Zach still has a choice—not like Mom. It's stupid for him to kill himself when he doesn't have to die."

Alan just looks at Joey. "Maybe," Alan says, "but maybe Zach doesn't have any more choice than Mom does about being sick."

Listening to Alan, I remember more about being back in the hospital that second time. I remember Dr. Curt talked to me about the new voices, helping me to understand about Dirtbag and Rat, the meanest bastards anywhere.

"These new, mean voices might come after you again—especially if you don't take your medicine. But if you're brave enough, Zach, you can fight them. You probably can't destroy them, but you can refuse to let them destroy you."

Dr. Curt's a nice guy, but he doesn't know everything. He doesn't know how bad Dirtbag and Rat can be, and I know that there's only one thing that's going to get rid of them for good! Only one thing that . . .

"Long gone . . . long gone . . . long gone . . ."

The phone rings and it's the cops. Alan talks to them. Actually he listens; all he says is "Good." Then he hangs up.

He turns to Joey and me and says, "Dr. Curtis is on his way."

Clearwater Hospital is about eighteen miles south of Spokane, so it's taking Dr. Curt a while to get here. I'm worried. I look at my watch. It's five oh three. I'm an hour and a half late for my medicine. I'm scared of Dirtbag and Rat. I need to think about something else—anything else.

"I have an idea," I say to Alan and Joey. "Do you guys think if we snuck out the back door real quietly, we could just get out of here? I could get my medicine and you wouldn't have to worry about jail and—"

Alan interrupts. "What?"

I ask again, "Could we just sneak out the back door and—"

Alan interrupts again. "What back door?"

I point to the closet and say, "The one in there."

Alan quickly goes over and opens the door to the little back room. He peeks inside.

"Jesus, Joey," Alan whispers excitedly. "There's a back way outa here!"

Joey says, "You kidding me?"

Alan answers, "No, for real, look at this!"

Joey hurries over and looks into the back room too.

Alan says, "Maybe the cops don't know about this. Maybe we can make a run for it."

I blurt out, "A run for your money . . ." although I'm not even sure what I mean or why I say it.

My head is starting to hurt real bad. It's a feeling I know too well.

But Alan smiles at me and says, "A run for our money, yeah."

19

Clinical note from Dr. Cal Curtis: Zachary Wahhsted's second hospitalization at Clearwater State Hospital:

Patient is depressed and upset. The two new voices "attacking" him are very difficult for him to deal with. They are cruel and hateful.

Diagnostic impression: A second psychotic break occurring so soon after the first with these suicidal impulses shows a severe psychosis. Zach's illness will be extraordinarily dangerous when stress and/or interruptions to his regular medication regimen occur.

"Long gone long gone long gone longgonelong-gonelonggone."

Everything begins to swirl—a terrible pain shoots across my forehead.

They're here.

"Hey, Wasteoid, time to die," Dirtbag whispers.

Rat laughs and screams, "*Yeah, time to die, Wasteoid!*"

Alan grabs me and pulls me toward the back door. Dirtbag and Rat circle me, whispering and screaming into my ears.

"*Time to die, Wasteoid!*"

"*Time to die!! Time to die!!*"

"Are you ready, Zach?"

I nod. Talking hurts too much.

We start out the back door, Alan first, now me, and Joey last, all of us bunched together. Alan and Joey are carrying their guns, holding them up like they could really shoot. The alley is dark.

Alan whispers, "We'll move slowly until we know it's okay."

"*You'll die slowly.*"

"*Yes, finally! Die, die, die!!*"

"If it's safe, if there aren't any cops, we'll run."

"*You can't run—you need to die!*"

"*Yes, yes!*"

"It'll be all right if we stick together. The cops don't know who is who . . ."

"*Kill the wasteoid, kill him good. . . .*"

". . . so even if they see us, they won't shoot. . . ."

"*Shoot the wasteoid, finally, YES . . .*"

time to die, Wasteoid

"Just stay close together. . . ."

Dirtbag says in his horrible voice, *"You know what we need here?"*

Rat screams, *"Blood, blood, we need wasteoid blood!"*

As we take our next steps into the dark alley, I can barely open my eyes. The world is all black and red, and I feel sick.

"DIEDIEDIEDIEDIEDIE."

"YOU NEED TO DIEDIEDIEDIEDIE."

Dirtbag says softly, *"You* know *you are worthless, Wasteoid. You* know *you are nothing, worm shit, a dead nothing—less than nothing, you are shit—you* gotta *end it all."*

Rat laughs, screaming, *"Yes, yes, yes . . . end it all!"*

Right now, this second, I *want* to end it all, once and for all, end it all. My body feels like it's on fire. I force my eyes open and see my reflection in the window of the door—flames lick my face, and my eyeballs melt down my cheeks—I quickly close my eyes again. When I force them open and look back at Joey, slimy bugs crawl out of his nose and ears, and when he opens his mouth to scream, his lips peel back and start to swallow him. . . .

My head feels like it's cracking in two. God, make it stop!

I shake all over, trying to catch a breath. Sweat pours from under my arms and down my chest and back. My tongue is thick. I hear nothing but the voices of Dirtbag and Rat. I'm like a bug stuck on a pin.

"Stop there!" a voice yells at us from out of the darkness.

I look up and see a man dressed in black. He's holding a rifle. Is he Dirtbag? Rat? I've never seen them before! Maybe they're not just voices. My god, maybe they're real!

"Halt!" the voice yells again.

Now another figure comes around the corner of the building, also dressed in black, his rifle at his shoulder. He yells, "Backup, position two!"

Alan and Joey swing around quickly and race back toward the coffee shop.

"Halt!"

"Kill them, slaughter them all!"

"Kill them! Kill them!!"

Alan and Joey race back through the door. I am alone. My head feels like it's splitting open.

"Kill him . . . KILL HIM!"

"KILL HIM!"

"Freeze or I'll shoot!"

"*Shoot!*"

"Wait, is he the hostage boy or one of the perps?"

"*Who cares, shoot him. . . . Kill him!!*"

"I don't know!"

"*Kill him NOW!!*"

"Does he have a weapon?"

"I can't tell!"

"Hold your fire!"

"*NO!!! FIRE, FIRE!!!!!*"

I think, yes, please, fire. Once and for all, please fire.

"*FIRE, FIRE, FIRE . . .*"

A second later someone grabs my shirt and pulls me from behind. Dirtbag and Rat are ripping me down to hell. I'm too weak to fight. I stumble backward, letting myself go.

There's a sharp cracking sound, and a bright blast of red and blue. . . . I hear someone cry out in pain.

My eyes are still closed tight. I can't tell *where* I am.

Now I'm falling into a chair. My head hurts so bad that I think it might explode for real.

When Dirtbag and Rat have me like this, all I

can do is to hold on and wait for them to go away. . . .
But I'm afraid that one day maybe they won't leave.

"Zach." I hear a voice calling to me. "Zach," the
voice says again. I force open my eyes, squinting to
keep the pain away. I see Alan's face.

I hear Joey's voice somewhere, calling Alan's name.
Joey sounds afraid.

"Zach." Alan's lips move, and I hear my name again.
"Are you okay?"

I try to answer, but words won't come.

Joey keeps calling to Alan over and over. But Alan
keeps asking, "Zach, are you all right?" He looks scared
and pale.

I manage to say, "Okay," softly.

Alan says, "You're okay? You're okay?"

I nod and realize that I'm telling the truth. As fast
as they came, Dirtbag and Rat are gone now.

I feel a cold wet spot on my chin where I've been
drooling. The top of my shirt is wet from drool too. My
armpits and chest and the back of my shirt are soaked
through with sweat. I feel like I might puke. My eyes
sting, like hot needles are being pulled out of them. My
skin feels raw.

Alan yells at me, "What the hell were you doing,

Zach? You kept yelling 'Die, die, die!' Were you trying to get yourself killed?"

I shake my head. I can't explain. I never can.

Joey stares at me from across the room.

Now Alan, who has been kneeling in front of me, sits back in a chair and closes his eyes. When he opens them, he looks down at the floor.

As I follow his eyes, at first I think I'm still seeing things, but now I realize why Joey is so scared. There is blood everywhere—bright, red blood splattered all across the floor.

20

Letter from Dr. Cal Curtis to Ms. Emily Wahhsted:

Zach's prognosis, truthfully, is not good. Schizophrenia is incurable. While medication increases a patient's ability to function, Zach is unlikely to ever achieve full self-care skills. I am sorry, of course, to have to report this, but to inform you otherwise would be unfair and inaccurate. . . .

"It got me through the hand. Straight through," Alan says, his left hand wrapped in a white towel, which is already soaked in blood and dripping onto the linoleum. I notice the streak of drops, some large, some smaller, that lead from the closet door, all the way across the room to where we're sitting.

"Oh, god," Joey says, tears in his eyes.

Alan says, very calmly, "It's okay, Joey, we're just back to plan one, waiting for Zach's shrink."

Joey starts, "But your hand, your—"

99

Blood, blood

Alan interrupts, standing up as he talks. "It doesn't even hurt that much. It did at first, but it's kind of numb now, I can barely feel—"

The phone rings.

Alan picks it up with his good hand and says, "Hello?" He listens, then says, "What the hell do you *think* we were doing? Trying to go home!"

There's another pause, a longer one. Then Alan answers, "Yeah, I got it. . . . You've made your point."

After another pause Alan says, "Put him on." Alan waits a few seconds, then says, "Hi, Dr. Curt."

Alan looks down at the phone and says, "Yeah, there is, there's a button right here for Speaker."

Alan pushes the button, and the next thing I hear is, "Can everybody hear me?" It's Dr. Curt's voice coming out over this tiny speaker in the phone. He sounds crackly and loud.

Joey and Alan both say, at the same time, "Yeah, we hear you."

I nod my head yes.

Alan looks at me and says, "He can't see you nod, Zach, you gotta say something."

Dr. Curt says, "Hi, Zach, how are you?"

I answer him, "I'm okay. Hungry. Kind of sleepy. Dirtbag and Rat have gone."

He asks, "They visited you?"

I say, "Yes."

Alan says, "Wait a minute, what're you talking about, Zach? No one's visited anybody—"

"Just a moment, Alan," Dr. Curt says, then, "Zach, they're gone now?"

I answer, "Yeah, they're gone."

"Good riddance, huh?" Dr. Curt says.

I think I smile as I answer, "Yeah."

I know I should say something about Alan's hand, about all the blood everywhere, but I can't think of the words.

Dr. Curt says, "The police won't let us go in there, Zach, but we're gonna get you out and get you your medicine as soon as we can, okay?"

"Okay," I say.

Alan says, "Dr. Curtis, if you'd just look at the promises they've made, we want to get Zach out of here, too. We all wanna get out of here."

Alan's voice sounds weak; he's breathing fast, and his words sound more like little grunts.

Dr. Curt says, "I'll read their agreement right away. Then give me a few minutes to talk to the police and I'll call you right back, all right?"

"Okay," Alan says.

Before Alan hangs up, I ask, "Does he know about the guns, Alan?"

Dr. Curt hears what I'm saying over the speakerphone and asks, "What about the guns?"

I start to answer, "Do you know about the bullets and—"

Alan interrupts me. "We'll tell him everything in a few minutes, okay, Zach?" While he's talking he puts the pointer finger of his good hand up to his lips in a signal for me to be quiet.

You know how people always do that, put that finger up in front of their lips like they could stop the words from coming out of their mouths? This never makes any sense to me, because it's always the other person they want to stop from talking, so how does putting their own finger in front of their own mouth do that? Still, since I know what the signal means, I shut up. I glance at Alan's other hand, the one wrapped in the bloody towel. It's lying on his lap, and now his jeans are bloody, too.

Alan turns back toward the phone speaker. "Call us when you're ready, okay, Dr. Curtis?"

"Okay," Dr. Curt says, and the phone goes dead.

"Jeez, Zach!" Joey immediately snaps at me. "What were you gonna do, tell 'em we didn't have any ammunition?"

I answer, "Just Dr. Curt."

"Damn!" Joey says, rushing over to me. He grabs the front of my shirt and pushes my face, hard, with the side of his gun. He doesn't really hit me with the gun, but the metal bumps hard against my lip and it hurts. He screams, "You idiot, don't you think the cops are listening?"

"Are they?" I ask. I mean it. I never thought of it.

"You're so stupid!" he yells, spit flying out of his mouth and into my face. He pulls his hand back to hit me, the hand with the gun in it, and starts to swing at my head.

I close my eyes and wait for the gun to smack me. After a few long seconds of waiting to get hit, it doesn't happen. I open my eyes and see Alan pulling Joey away.

Joey yells, "I'm sick of this retard! All day he's messed us up. He should have killed himself back when he had the chance."

Alan says, "Shut up, Joey, just shut your goddamned mouth!"

The two brothers stand frozen, staring at each other. After a few seconds Joey lowers his arm and Alan lets go of Joey's wrist.

The towel around Alan's hand slips down suddenly, almost falling off. Alan winces as he grabs it, cradling his hurt hand in his good one. I can see, for just a second, the place where the bullet has gone through Alan's palm. It looks terrible. The hole looks red and sore and like hamburger before it's cooked.

Alan looks at me and says, his voice tired, "It's okay, Zach." He glances at my lip. "Are you hurt?"

I reach up and touch my mouth with my finger. It's bleeding a little. I answer, "My lip hurts."

Joey yells, "If you'd learn to shut your stupid mouth . . ." His face is almost as red as Alan's hand. He turns away and just stares at the wall.

Alan looks at me and says, "Joey's right about the cops listening when we talk to Dr. Curtis. You need to just be quiet when we're talking, okay?"

I nod.

Alan is still looking at me. "Zach, who are Dirtbag and Rat?"

I don't answer.

"No one was here before except us."

I say nothing.

Alan doesn't say anything for a second either. Then he asks, "You can't tell what's real, can you, Zach?"

I ask Alan, "But you're real, right?"

Joey yells, "Look at his hand, moron! He got that saving you!" Joey makes a mumbled, angry sound and says, "I'd have let 'em blow your head off!"

Alan ignores Joey and says to me, "Yeah, Zach, I'm real." As he talks, he carefully rewraps the bloody towel around his hand, squinching his face each time the towel goes across the wound. When he's done, he looks over at me. "This is all real."

I ask Alan, "Your guns are real, too, right? Only they won't shoot except for when Joey shot the drawer."

Alan says, "Yeah, the guns are real, all of this is real. But what if I'm lying? You're never sure about anything, are you?"

I think about it for a second, then answer honestly, "I guess not really, nope."

Joey says to Alan, "What's Zach being an idiot have to do with us? He's a retard!"

Alan says, "No, he's not a retard, Joey; that's just it." Alan pauses a second, thinking, then says, "Zach's brain is all upside down and inside out, but he's not a retard—"

Joey interrupts, "Retard. Crazy. What's the differ ence? He's messed us up all day."

Alan sighs. He looks at me as he walks over to Joey.

"Listen," Alan says to him. "We're in trouble here, I know that, but we'll get out of it sooner or later— Zach is *never* going to get out of what's happening to him. Man, I'd rather be us any day."

21

Letter from Ms. Emily Wahhsted to Dr. Cal Curtis:

Thank you for your honesty about Zach. Once you've seen your only child with a rifle in his mouth, it can't get a whole lot worse, except, of course, for the possibility that one day I might not get home in time. . . .

The phone rings.

Alan picks it up. "Hello," he says, then "Okay." He presses the phone's speaker button again.

I hear Dr. Curt's voice. "Can you all hear me?" he asks.

Alan and Joey both say yes.

I nod my head again. I'm not supposed to talk 'cause the cops are listening.

Alan says, "Zach's all right, we can all hear you."

Dr. Curt explains that he has read the cops' agreement and that it looks all right.

Alan asks Dr. Curt, "You sure?"

Dr. Curt answers, "Well, I'm not a lawyer, Alan, but even if they wanted to lie, we have everything in writing. They can't go back on it."

Alan takes a deep breath. He looks around the coffee shop. I follow his eyes. There's the stack of tablecloths in a cupboard in the corner and some boxes of plastic and Styrofoam cups. I hear the hum of the freezer from the little closet room. Below where Alan is standing there's a puddle of blood from his towel bandage, and there's the other blood splattered in different-sized drops all across the floor.

Finally Alan turns to Joey and says. "That's it, Joey, it's over."

Joey shrugs. "Okay."

Alan turns and says to the speakerphone, "Okay, Dr. Curtis, tell the police we're coming out; we give up. Also, tell them, please, that our guns aren't loaded." Alan pauses a second and looks down at his hand. "We're coming out now, we give up, but I'm gonna need a doctor."

wing-wong

22

Clinical note by Dr. Cal Curtis:

In the years that I have worked with Zach,
he has progressed to the point where
he usually copes pretty well with his
illness. He still struggles to understand
"reality," and in ways this can make him
seem "retarded." Zach has an above-average
I.Q., but the limitations of his illness
make it difficult for him to understand
when he is in danger. . . .

My lip has stopped bleeding but is kind of puffy. It feels weird.

I'm walking in front as the three of us move across the coffee shop to the front door. The windows of the coffee shop are all sparkly with the big spotlights the police are shining in on us. When I reach the front door of the coffee shop, I pull it toward me and the little bell goes *tingaling*. We walk out.

Alan and Joey are crouching down right behind me. I guess they're still not sure the police won't shoot them. We move slowly. It's dark out, but all the police cars are lined up next to each other, their lights flashing, and cops squat down behind the cars with shotguns and handguns pointed right at us.

Some people are standing way back, behind some yellow tape. I wonder if my mom is back there. I guess she's worried for me, 'cause that's what moms do.

"JUST STEP FORWARD SLOWLY, BOYS, AND NOBODY WILL GET HURT!" the big microphone voice booms out.

"Okay!" I yell back, and I notice several of the cops jerk at the sound of my voice. I'm used to having guns pointed at me by now, so I don't care. But I wonder if the cops' guns have bullets in them.

I yell, "Do you guys have any bullets?"

There's a pause for a second, then the microphone guy yells, "DON'T WORRY ABOUT THAT— EVERYTHING IS FINE!"

I yell, "Good," back to him, but the truth is, I can't stop thinking about everything that's happened in these last hours: Frosty and Stormy . . . I mean Alan and Joey . . . Laurel and Hardy . . . the old ladies . . . and that little girl's mom touching my arm and how pretty she was . . .

"*Wing-wong—happy dong—wing-wong—happy dong.*"

"Up yours," I say to the voice.

gong-wong

"NOW, SON, JUST STAY CALM, YOU'RE DOIN' FINE."

Alan, behind me, whispers, "Just be quiet, Zach, all right?"

I say, "Sure."

"LAY YOUR WEAPONS DOWN AND SLIDE THEM AWAY FROM YOU, THEN LIE FACE-DOWN ON THE GROUND."

I don't have a weapon. My clothes will get all dirty if I lie down. I didn't try to rob the coffee shop!

I yell to the microphone voice, "Why do *I* have to lie on the ground?"

I hear Alan's voice behind me again. "Just do it, Zach."

I look back at Alan. He and Joey are already lying down. They push their guns away from them. Little sparks fly off the black gun as it slides along the pavement. In another second Alan and Joey lie all flat out like pancakes on the cement. I can't help but laugh.

The cops don't laugh, though. They still have all their guns pointed right at us . . . at me, actually.

I think again about everything that's happened: Alan's face with the slivers in it and his hand bleeding onto the floor and Joey getting mad and hitting me and Dirtbag and Rat showing up and the little girl peeing her dress and . . . suddenly I remember!!

I spin around quickly to go back into the coffee shop. I have to slow down a little to make sure I don't step on Joey or accidentally kick Alan's hurt hand.

"HOLD YOUR FIRE!!" the microphone voice yells.

"STOP!"

"HOLD YOUR FIRE!"

I keep moving, push the coffee-shop door open, and race back inside.

When I come back out, just a minute later, the police are putting Joey in handcuffs and holding Alan by his arms. A policeman rushes up to grab me, too, but he stops when he sees the three maple bars I'm holding, one for Alan, one for Joey, and one for me.

"What's wrong with you, boy—you almost got yourself killed!" he says. He sounds mad.

A moment later my mom pushes him out of the way. He spins around toward Mom, but Dr. Curt steps between them.

"Hold on," Dr. Curt says.

The policeman says, "I have to take him. We need to interrogate him."

Dr. Curt says, "No, you don't, not unless you want every TV station in town showing you jerking around a sick kid." Dr. Curt nods at some men with TV cameras racing toward us. "Really," Dr. Curt says calmly to the policeman, "take it easy, officer. It's okay. Relax. This kid needs his medication. You can have him in just a minute."

I look at the policeman, and he takes a deep breath. I've seen Dr. Curt talk this same way to patients in the hospital about a million times. The cop shrugs his shoulders and turns away.

Mom gives me a big hug. I'm not too crazy about hugs, but if it makes her feel better, I guess it's all right. I try not to get any maple bar on her.

Dr. Curt steps over to the police and Alan and Joey. They're all talking, although Joey's not saying much. More people from around the parking lot rush forward now, and the guys with TV cameras start to shove them in my face. Everybody stares at me. Mom puts her arm around me and says to the TV people, "My son is a minor, and you have no release or permission to show his image on the air. . . . I can't wait to see you try it. . . ."

In about two seconds, all the TV cameras turn away from us and start to follow Alan and Joey. Suddenly a skinny lady steps through the rest of the people and walks right up to Alan and Joey.

Joey looks up and bursts into tears. He says, "I'm sorry, Mom."

The lady puts her arm around him, and he hides his face against her shoulder.

Alan is fighting back his tears, his lower lip shaking. "I'm sorry, too, Mama," he says. "It's all my fault."

Their mom reaches out with her other arm, and Alan steps toward her. All the police stand back and let Alan and Joey's mom hug her sons. She has tears in her eyes. Of course, I don't know how she feels, but she doesn't look mad. She whispers some things to Alan and Joey, and after a couple seconds Alan actually smiles a little bit and Joey takes a couple of real deep breaths, then stops crying. Joey lifts his head up. The three of them, surrounded by the cops, start to walk toward the police cars and an ambulance.

Dr. Curt walks back over to me and asks, "How you doin,' Zach?"

I answer, "I don't know." It's the truth.

Dr. Curt says to me, "You did very well today."

"I did?"

"Yes. You helped all those other hostages earlier, and you helped Alan and Joey. Everyone appreciates what you did."

Without even thinking that I'm going to say it, suddenly the words just fly out of my mouth. "Can I have all three of these maple bars then?"

The reason I ask is that it doesn't look like Alan and Joey can have theirs; they're already leaving.

My mom smiles and hugs me again. "Yes, Zach," she says.

I wonder if the president of the United States of America gets all the maple bars he wants anytime he wants them. I wonder what the ocean would look like if they emptied out all the water and filled it up with the stuff they put on top of maple bars.

"Gong-wong, wong-gong.

"Gong-wong—wong-gong . . ."

"Zach," Mom says, "here you go." She holds out my medicine with a bottle of water. I hand Dr. Curt my maple bars, gulp down my pills real fast, and then grab the treats back.

I glance at my watch. It's late. I want to go home.

I look over at Alan and Joey and their mom one last time. Alan looks back at me, too. They all stop walking, and now all three of them are looking at me. I wave good-bye. Joey turns away, but Alan nods his head. Their mom smiles at me and says, "Thank you."

I say, "You're welcome, thanks for coming." Then

I almost add, "Have a nice day," but even I know that would be inappropriate.

I take a huge bite of maple bar . . . ummmmm . . . perfect!
Time to go home.

23

Three months later . . .

Mender Brothers Sentenced as Juveniles: Coffee Siege Ends with a Deadly Twist

By Kelly Hillstead, Correspondent, *Spokane Intelligencer*

SPOKANE—After months of mental evaluations and a firestorm of public controversy, Alan and Joseph Mender, 17 and 14, were sentenced today to nine months in juvenile detention and two years' probation after their attempted holdup of Sunshine Espresso on North Francis last October.

Defense attorneys insisted the brothers were driven to desperation by the burden of their mother's cancer diagnosis and costly treatments. Opponents lambasted the light sentence, insisting it sent a misleading message to other teens.

In a tragic twist, Zachary Wahhsted, a teen hostage and apparent hero of the coffee-shop saga, committed suicide at his mother's home just a week ago.

According to Dr. Calvin Curtis, who also testified on the Mender brothers' behalf, 16-year-old Wahhsted had struggled for several years with schizophrenia. This disease is a chemical brain disorder that frequently leaves victims haunted by phantom voices and unable to define or deal with reality as we know it.

"It was a good day for the Mender boys," Curtis said in a telephone interview, "but the death of Zach certainly casts a dark shadow over it. For Zach to have survived all the dangers of the holdup only to die by his own hand, a victim of the dangers inside himself, is tragic. Unfortunately, deaths like Zach's are all too common in patients suffering from schizophrenia," Curtis concluded. "Zachary Wahlsted was a good kid who had a terrible illness. He was much beloved; he'll be missed."

. . . end it all

If you'd like to know more about Terry Trueman, visit his web site at www.truemannews.com. If you'd like to know more about schizophrenia, click on the button for "issues."

Also by Terry Trueman

Hc 0-06-028519-2 • Pb 0-06-447213-2

A PRINTZ HONOR BOOK

Shawn McDaniel is an enigma and a miracle—except no one knows it, least of all his father. His life is not what it may seem to be to anyone looking at him. Not even those who love him best have any idea of what he is truly like. In this extraordinary and powerful first novel, the reader learns to look beyond the obvious and finds a character whose spirit is rich beyond imagining and whose story is unforgettable.

Paul McDaniel has everything going for him: looks, brains, and enough talent on the basketball court to take him just about any-where. His brother, on the other hand, has nothing—not even a working brain. How can Paul pursue his own happiness when his brother will never know any-thing but meaningless pain from his illness? Dangerously con-sumed by his rage and guilt, Paul must face his demons if he wants any kind of future at all.

Hc 0-06-623960-5

HarperTempest
An Imprint of HarperCollinsPublishers

www.harpertempest.com   www.terrytrueman.com